Jethro

"Joe Roberts" Caputo

Published by "Joe Roberts" Caputo, 2024.

Table of Contents

Chapter 1: The Road to Nowhere 1
Chapter 2: Searching for Jethro 11
Chapter 3: Encounters in the Ozarks 23
Chapter 4: The Quiet Charm of Priscilla 37
Chapter 5: Whispers in the Wilderness 49
Chapter 6: The Phantom's Promise 59
Chapter 7: A Union of Promises 73
Chapter 8: The Turning Point 87
Chapter 9: City of Dreams 97
Chapter 10: New Beginnings 111
Chapter 11: The Guardians' Ultimatum 123
Epilogue: Legacy of the Guadian of the Ozarks 133

My profound gratitude to my son Phillip, for his patience and creativity in making this book a reality.

Copyright © 2024 by "Joe Roberts" Caputo

All rights reserved. No part of this publication may be reproduced, distributed, or transmitted in any form or by any means, including photocopying, recording, or other electronic or mechanical methods, without the prior written permission of the publisher, except in the case of brief quotations embodied in critical reviews and certain other noncommercial uses permitted by copyright law.

For permission requests, please contact the publisher at: joeroberts3385@gmail.com.

Chapter 1: The Road to Nowhere

Maxwell S. Longfellow was pissed—pure and simple. After working for and obtaining a $200,000 journalism diploma from Yale, all he had to show for it was a $200,000 journalism diploma from Yale. For 12 years, he had a job, not a career, at a second-tier newspaper in Grand Rapids, Michigan. Michigan! "I'm a Boca guy, for God's sake. What the hell am I doing in this God-forsaken wilderness where I am always cold?" His life had taken a turn for the worse these past six months, and he wanted a change. He longed to do gonzo journalism like some war correspondents or Hemingway but was relegated to doing puff pieces for celebrities and "influencers." His on-again, off-again relationship with Doris, the mousy secretary to the publisher (who happened to be her father), was off again, and he wondered if this time would be the last time they would "take a break."

"Everything is so damn stale," he complained. "Even these lousy cigarettes taste... lousy," he said as he stabbed it to death in an ashtray that already had seven or eight 2-inch-long victims.

His nerves were shot, too. He couldn't sleep much. When he was able to get a few hours of sleep, the dreams were not good—unfulfilled promises for a guy with a 147 IQ. Every time he remembered that number, he laughed derisively.

"A hell of a lot of good all that brainpower does me," he thought. "Maybe if I was taller," he mused uselessly. But he wasn't. He was 5'6" and 143 pounds of minimal masculinity. His features were regular—neither handsome nor homely. Small nose, small mouth, small eyes, which were... brown. Not hazel "with golden flecks in the right light." No. Brown. Regular, muddy... brown. His hair was straight and also... brown. Not chestnut. Nope. Brown. He wore rimless glasses that made him appear older than his 32 years. He dressed in suits that were well-made but ill-fitting, giving the impression of a person who had money but didn't know how to spend it correctly. He even took to wearing a gray fedora. He lived on Hot Pockets, pizza, with an occasional foray into the land of the health-conscious, Taco Bell. Of course, this necessitated his having an ample supply of antacids, which he popped regularly. But lately, he could barely nibble a Nacho Chalupa, and he was done. He lived in a one-bedroom apartment on the west side of town, about 15 minutes from the Grand Rapids

Gazette. Can you believe a smart guy like him working at a Gazette? The newspaper was one of the oldest in the city and prided itself on the history of the paper that had its beginnings right after the Civil War. Fat chance of changing the name now. Yes, everything was stale and tasteless, and he didn't see any change on the horizon. But there had to be one. He could not go through life like this. He needed a change, some excitement. But he was stuck on this never-ending treadmill that never went anywhere.

Just when he thought things couldn't go deeper into the toilet, his editor called him in for a crazy assignment.

Stan Grubins was a big man. Well, he was a very fat man. Tipping a tortured scale at 330 pounds, he moved his six-foot bulk around like a steam shovel, moving slowly so as not to knock over anything not nailed down. The fact that he was clumsy didn't help his appearance, which always consisted of stains from foods from his last meal, which was never the last, but one continuous nibbling on a pretzel, a donut, peanuts. Fruit? Ugh. Strangely, he had a small head. Well, it was probably regular-sized, except on that massive frame, it looked like a small balloon. For a 70-year-old man, he had a thatch of thick, white hair and an equally bushy white mustache. His moon face had a bulbous nose, fat lips, but remarkably beautiful gray eyes. The eyes are what caught people off guard. Just when they were ready to dispatch him into the region of the detestable, they saw those eyes, and they were... kind? But that couldn't be! The man was a tyrant and the bane of the existence of all six of the employees at the Gazette. When he wasn't yelling, he was growling. Today he was growling.

"Longfellow. Get your ass in here!"

Max had mixed feelings. First, he thought he was getting fired. Then he thought, "Damn, I bet he won't fire me."

"Yes, boss?"

"This paper has been stuck in neutral for months."

"Uh... yeah?"

"So, we need to shake things up."

"O... OK?"

"I heard a story about this kid, well they're not sure if he is a kid or not. Anyway, people claim he can talk to animals and plants and stuff."

"So?"

"So, I want you to go out there and check it out."

"Where is this... kid?"

"In the Ozarks."

"The Ozarks? Boss, that takes in a lot of territory."

"What do you mean?"

"Well, they take in the mountain ranges of Missouri, Arkansas, and Oklahoma. If I remember my geography, I think it takes in part of Kansas."

"Mmm, I didn't know that," grumbled the boss.

"Still, it would make for a good story. 'The search for the boy who talks to the animals.' Hell, we could run a series. You could start out searching for him and file daily reports of where you've been, who you talked to, that kind of stuff. Get some colorful interviews with old geezers sitting in general stores. Yeah, this could be a circulation builder. Maxwell, you will finally get that byline you have been bugging me about."

"Boss, I'm not so sure. You think those people are going to talk to a runt like me? Maybe you should send Luke."

"Luke?? Are you crazy? He can barely tie his shoes without wondering how he did it. He is big and brawny and dumb as a stump. I have to keep him on, or my sister Della would have a fit."

"Boss, how did a beautiful girl like Della get hooked up with a dolt like Jake?"

"I would hate to be coarse, but from what I see in those tight jeans of his, he has a package that can challenge a horse. Get my drift?"

"Uh... oh. Yes. Yes. I... I get it."

"Why do you think she always has a smile on her face?"

"Uh... boss, I'm not comfortable talking about such things."

"Yeah, well neither am I. I have nightmares thinking of that animal mounting my little Della...."

"Boss, please!"

"OK. OK. back to business. No, it has to be you. You have the damn vocabulary and imagination to weave a story. Start doing some research. You leave on Monday."

"Monday? Boss, it's already Wednesday."

"Then you had better move your ass and get cracking. The more I think about it, the more excited I get about this story. This is your big chance, Maxwell. Don't blow it."

"I... I'll try...," he said as he crept out of the office.

When he got to his desk, he sat down heavily in his chair that had a tear in the leather fabric and caught on his pants every time he sat down. But he was unaware of his pants or his seat or anything but... the Ozarks! What the hell am I going to do in the Ozarks? Then it hit him. Square in his small, unassuming face. You idiot! You wanted a change. You wanted some excitement. Well, here it is on a platter. The boss already knows that this search can take a while and take you to a lot of different places. Isn't that what you wanted? And on his dime! No, this is exactly an answer to your prayers if you were the praying kind. The more Max thought about it, the more excited he got. First thing, hit the Internet and see what he could find. 'God bless Google,' he thought.

He jotted down some facts and then mapped out an itinerary that would methodically eliminate certain areas, according to intelligence he could glean from people he met that might have some knowledge of this kid. With this full head of steam, he marched into his boss's office and said, "Boss, are you prepared for how much this search might cost?"

The big man, not having something to chew on, was chomping on a big cigar. "What?" he asked irritably.

"I said, are you prepared for how much it might cost for this search? I mean, I will probably have to travel to several states. Room and board and that kind of stuff."

"I don't give a flying crap! Do what you have to do. File an expense report. I'll have a Mastercard made out that has sufficient funds for you to do whatever you need to do. Get this done, Maxwell, and you may be looking at a Pulitzer and this paper doubling its circulation."

"OK, boss. Just wanted to clear the decks."

The more Max thought about it, the more excited he got. Because he already established that the Ozarks take in such a great swath of land, and there is no way to know where this kid might be, this journey could take months. But, just like war correspondents, he would file daily reports from wherever he was, talking to whomever he could. In the process, he was sure he could pick up some stories he could weave into a tapestry of what Middle America is like.

He knew he had a knack for describing things colorfully. Couple that with the ongoing suspense of hunting for the elusive "Boy from the Ozarks." He already decided that was what he would call his series. 'Hey, there even could be a book here. Maybe a movie. Wow! Throttle it down, Max.' But the exhilaration he felt was something he had not felt in a long time.

The next couple of days, he gathered what he considered essentials for his trek. He decided on minimalizing. Instead of a stack of shirts he normally would pack, he opted for a few of the new wash-and-wear shirts that can be rinsed the night before, and by the next morning, would be fresh as a daisy and ready to go. Same with underwear. Also, with jeans. Two pairs were sufficient along with a couple of pairs of chinos and one good pair of dress slacks, in case he was invited to dinner somewhere. One tie. One dress shirt. Period. A couple of sweaters of varying thickness, a windbreaker, and an overcoat. In the interest of the adventure, he bought a wide-brimmed hat à la Harrison Ford and Indiana Jones. When he tried it on, he found it was surprisingly heavy, but the looks he got from female passersby confirmed his thought about a little badass not being a bad thing. Two pairs of heavy hiking boots, along with his Jordans and a pair of dress loafers, and socks of all kinds, and he was set. Hell, if he needed anything, he could buy it with his Mastercard.

As a matter of fact, that night, he paid a visit to his quasi-fiancée wearing the hat.

When Doris opened the door, she did a double take.

"Max? Is that you?"

"Nobody else, baby," he said out of the corner of his mouth. Why he said that and the way he said it was beyond him, but he liked the effect it had on his tremulous girl.

He stamped into the room, plopped onto a couch, and kept his hat on.

"Think a guy could get a beer in this joint?" he asked, staying in a character he was making up on the spot.

"Y... yes. Of... course. Yes. Right away, Max."

She scurried to the fridge and brought back a can of Bud Light. She even pulled the tab for him.

"Listen, sweets, I'll be leaving town soon."

"Leaving? Where are you going?"

"Your father has this crazy idea that I should track down this kid who can talk to animals or something. Anyway, he lives somewhere in the Ozarks, and I have been ordered to go out and get his story."

"Uh... where in the Ozarks?" she asked, interested.

"Babe, it could be anywhere from Missouri to Kansas, with Oklahoma and Arkansas thrown in for good measure."

"B...But, how will you know where to look?"

"Logic, sweetheart. Logic. I have maps of the entire region. I intend to start at the foot of the Ozark mountains. Probably start in St. Louis and work my way south. The whole area takes in almost 50,000 square miles. So, this is a daunting task, and I don't know how long it may take me to find this kid—if I ever do. But, in a way, it doesn't really matter. The suspense of my trek through Middle America will make for good copy. I will be sending daily reports of what I saw that day, the folks I might have spoken with, and stories they might have about the mountains. Actually, the longer I am away in different places, the more the suspense will build until I finally corner this kid."

"Max, you could be gone for... months!" she said worriedly.

"That's about the size of it, Toots."

"Toots? What has come over you, Max?"

"I'm just facing facts. Cards on the table."

"What about... us?"

"Doris, there hasn't been much of 'us' for a while. Be honest."

"Well, there have been extenuating circumstances and..."

"Yeah, yeah, blah, blah. Face it, baby, the spark is gone. I suggest you look around for some guy who is down with all of your little eccentricities."

"Eccentricities?"

"C'mon, Doris. Every time you sit down at a table, you need to arrange the salt and pepper shaker just right. You wipe every knife and fork with a napkin. You won't take a sip of any fluid from a glass or bottle I have drunk from without boiling it to within an inch of its life."

She said defensively, "Well, a person can't be too careful with germs and such."

"Yeah. You were right in your element with the pandemic of 2020. Man, you couldn't get enough of that spray, could you?"

"Well, we were told to take precautions and..."

"Yeah, and you took that and ran with it. Why, I remember you carrying a spray and spritzing my car seats before you got in. Damn, I hated that smell."

"Well, we had to protect…"

"Sure. And what happened? You got the vaccine plus two boosters and you still got Covid. Twice."

"It's just that I was around a lot of people, and we passed it around."

"Hey, remember, I wasn't holed up in some ivory tower somewhere. I was in the trenches reporting on the whole thing. And, Doris, what happened?"

"What do you mean?" she asked petulantly.

"I'm asking what happened to me and other Neanderthals who refused to get the vaccine?"

"I… I don't know what you mean," she said evasively.

"Yes, you do. We didn't get Covid. No, we didn't, and that pissed you off."

"Nonsense. And you know how I don't like crude language," she sniffed.

"Yeah, well, put that on the list of do's and don'ts for the next guy."

"Are you… breaking up with me?" she asked incredulously.

"Doris, when was the last time we slept together?"

"What?"

"Simple question."

"I… I don't keep track of such things," she said stiffly.

"You would if it was great. It wasn't. Ergo, no remembrance."

"I hate it when you use those words."

"Hey, I can't help it if the 147 slips out from time to time."

"You know, Max, sometimes you can be a… a…"

"Go ahead and say it, Doris. It might make you feel better."

"Bitch! There. I said it."

"Again. With feeling, please," he said with maddening calm.

"BITCH! BITCH! How is that?" she asked heatedly.

"Better. How do you feel?"

Slightly pink from the effort, she had to admit, it felt good.

"See? Once in a while, you should let off some steam."

She was breathing heavily now, and she had a strange look in her eyes.

"Doris?"

"Come with me."

"Where?"

"To bed."

"But, I'm not sleepy and... oh... oh!"

"Sleep is the last thing on my mind right now. I thought I would give you a proper sendoff."

It had been weeks since their last encounter, so he was a little randy, and he took her hand and followed her to the bedroom. She dimmed the lights, disrobed, and slipped under the covers. He followed suit and was about to join her when she whispered hoarsely, "Lose the boxers, but keep the hat."

He complied, and for the next hour, she wore him out.

After the third go-round, he begged for mercy.

"Doris, where the hell did this come from?"

"Any complaints?" she asked coyly.

"No! No. None at all. Not a bit," he answered hurriedly.

"Now, get your things and get out," she demanded coldly.

"Doris!"

"Mission accomplished. I gave you something to think about during your travels. I may be here when you get back, but in your parlance, 'I wouldn't make book on it.'"

So, Max gathered his stuff, shimmied into his pants, and left her grinning. The last thing he heard her say was, "Damn, I sure could use a cigarette!"

Licking his wounds all the way to his car, he had to grin and admire Doris for her pluck.

"Maybe, I was a bit hasty," he thought. "Oh, well, too late now." He had a mission, and he was ready to go.

After goodbyes to the staff and last-minute instructions from the boss, Max set off on his quest. He decided to use the company's van. He emptied it of cables and various equipment, although he took a good quality video camera to chronicle some sights he would see along the way.

The night before, he mapped out a course on a huge Hagstrom map, which seemed archaic now, but it was perfect for his purposes. It was big enough to keep sprawled out on the seat, and quick glances could assure him he was on the right track. He really had no idea how to begin. He guessed the best place would be where this lad was seen last. But that was of little help. It seemed he moved around the Ozark Mountains, apparently as the spirit moved him. However, Max had heard he was spotted once just south of St. Louis. So, that was as good a place to start as any. Armed with a bunch of CDs, hat on head, he began.

Chapter 2: Searching for Jethro

The first couple of hundred miles were interesting as Max tried out the video camera and found, while it was a bit cumbersome, it produced excellent video with high-quality audio. His first stop was at a quaint general store. The log cabin appearance was just as rustic inside as outside. The caretaker was a colorful old man of around 70 years. Small but spry, he was glad for any visitors, and Max was greeted with a big smile and a hearty, "Howdy, stranger. Isaiah Johnson at your service."

"Hi. Nice place you have here. Seems like you have a little of everything."

The white-haired man was thin but fit, standing around 5'7".

"That's kind of why we call it a 'General Store,'" he said with an impish grin.

"Touche," Max whispered.

"Parle-vous français?"

Max was shocked that this old guy in nowheresville actually knew some French.

"No. No. I really don't. I just show off from time to time, but you called my bluff."

"Oh, I was stationed over there toward the end of Desert Storm. Don't ask me how they thought I could be of any use there, but I was in intelligence, and they needed some code breakers. I was pretty good with codes back in the day."

"Can you write code?"

"No. No. That stuff is way beyond me. I can work my way around a computer for ordinary stuff, but that's about it."

Max liked this man. He was good-looking for an old guy. On a whim, he explained what his mission was.

"You haven't heard anything about this kid who can, you know, talk to animals and such?"

"Oh, there are tales about some kid who was raised by wolves or something. But, I think it's more folklore than anything."

"But, you HAVE heard of him?" Max insisted.

"These are the Ozarks. You hear all kinds of things."

"I wonder if you would mind if I videotaped a little conversation with you? They are running a series in a newspaper I work for back in Grand Rapids."

"Video? Do you think you might get a shot of my sign in the shot?"

Max had to admire the resourcefulness of this old guy.

"Sure. Why not?"

Max unpacked the camera, checked the light, and found it was sufficient. He switched it on and narrated a brief introduction about where he was and who he was about to speak with.

The old guy seemed to warm to the whole deal and smiled throughout the conversation, which not only touched on the boy but added some colorful facts about that part of the country. After about ten minutes, Max snapped off the camera.

"Thank you, Isaiah. That was great."

"That was fun. Any chance I might get to see it sometime?"

"To be honest, I really don't know what they will do with this, but if it's possible to get a cassette for you, I will. Can I take one of these cards?"

"Absolutely. And take some of these pecans with you, too. They make for a good snack when you are driving."

"Thanks. What do I owe you?"

"Oh, nothing. You just made my day. When I get home, my wife will die of envy that I was on TV."

"Well, I'm not sure..."

"Hey, she doesn't know that. There was a video camera. That's good enough. Thanks."

"Thanks, Isaiah. Take it easy."

"Good luck," said the smiling old man.

Chewing on some of the most delicious pecans he had ever tasted, Max resumed his journey until it got dark. He pulled into a Motel Six, took his camera in with him, and locked the van up tight.

Once he had ordered some burgers and fries from the simple cafeteria, he looked over the footage he had taken. Before leaving, he got a stack of pre-addressed and stamped padded mailing envelopes. He videotaped himself, giving some interesting details of his day and the sights he had seen. His capacity to describe things vividly came into play here, and he found that he was quite comfortable with off-the-cuff remarks. He decided that the narrative would be told like a story, with as few boring details as possible.

After watching a little TV, he found he was quite tired and hit the sack around 11.

After a shower and breakfast at the motel, Max, armed with a jug of coffee, set out again. He had plotted the day's trip to include a trip along the Merrimac River to a place called Old Mines. Max didn't know what he might find, but it sounded interesting. Besides, river scenes were always pleasant to see, and since this was June, the weather was sunny and bright. He made several stops along the way, having coffee and a buttered roll at an old diner. Max liked diners. Doris hated them. He liked the smell of coffee that was almost palpable when you opened the door. He slid onto a red leatherette stool, and a tall waitress named Beatrice asked, "What will you have?" in a southern accent.

"Beatrice, is it?"

"That's what the name badge says," she said with a smile that was friendly but indicated that there was no time for platitudes.

"Do you have pancakes?"

"Best in the Ozarks. How many would you like?"

"Oh, maybe three or four. And maybe, some sausage?"

"Coffee?"

"Yes, please."

He didn't mean for it to sound so urgent.

"You driving a lot?"

"H...how...?"

"Been doing this for a long time. I can tell when someone has been on the road for a while."

Max estimated that she was in her mid-40s. Specks of gray could be seen in a full head of auburn hair that fell to her shoulders.

Max was a little surprised that her hair did not have a net.

"You surprised that I don't wear a net?"

"I... I... uh... didn't..." Max sputtered.

"I hate nets. I own part of this place, so, it's no net."

"Beatrice, if I had hair as pretty as yours, I wouldn't want to hide it under some ugly net."

"Well, aren't you the charmer."

That was the first time Max had ever been called "a charmer."

'Must be the hat,' he thought.

"Sure wasn't like that Gestapo during the pandemic."

"Really?"

"Yeah, they were breaking chops about us not having enough spray stuff and wraps and that kind of stuff. They were threatening to shut us down. Luckily a couple of truckers overheard the conversation and came over.

"Trouble, Beatrice?"

"The guy from the government is threatening to shut me down because I don't meet requirements."

Now, these two guys were big, beefy guys. They had their wool caps on, and between them, they made the government man look like a toad. They got on either side of him, and I could see he was scared to death.

"Listen, government man. Me and my trucker friends drive a long way delivering goods to folks. We look forward to coming here for some coffee, the best chili anywhere, and great pie. Let me tell you, that thought keeps us going that last hundred miles. If we didn't have that short little rest and good food, not to mention good conversation, we would get downright ornery. Do you catch my drift, government man?"

"I... I suppose we could put this under... uh... extenuating circumstances," he muttered fearfully.

"You do that. What's your name?"

"W...why do you want to know?"

"Just want to know who to come after if anything happens to Beatrice. And, we WILL come find you. Trust me on this."

The threat almost had the poor man pissing his pants.

"That won't be necessary. I promise. Really."

"Good. Beatrice, get him a bowl of chili and put it on my tab."

"I still smile every time I remember that," the tall woman smiled.

"Where you headed?"

Max explained what he was about, and he was surprised that Beatrice, too, had heard of the boy.

"Get a lot of truckers here, and some of them claimed that they saw this boy/man in blue overalls walking in a field. He seemed to be alone except for a dog who was at his heels. Although some of the truckers could have sworn it was a gray wolf. But, as soon as he heard the trucks, he ducked back into the forest."

"Wow. That's fascinating, Beatrice. Thank you for that information. That will make for a nice part of my daily report. Would you mind if I used your name?"

"Sure, as long as you spell it right."

"I will, and thanks."

The cook cried, "Cakes, up!"

Beatrice brought him a 12-inch platter with pancakes that filled the entire plate.

"Wow. Those are whoppers," Max cried.

"Go big or go home," Beatrice quipped.

She offered several syrups and copious amounts of butter that Max spread generously between the slabs. There were three fat sausages on the side. Max cut into one of them, and the skin burst. He took a bite and closed his eyes.

"My God, that is delicious!"

"Try the flapjacks."

Max did, and he swore that these were the best he had ever tasted, and he was a devotee of IHOP and Denny's, but these were out of sight.

"How could they be so good?"

"Buttermilk," was the cryptic reply.

"Buttermilk," Max echoed. "I'll be damned. Of course, now I am spoiled for anything else."

"Well, we've been here for 24 years. You come back."

"You know, if I can, I certainly will, Beatrice."

"Want me to top off that coffee?"

"Read my mind."

"Like I said, been doing this a long time. Want me to fill your jug?"

"Beatrice, if I was a foot taller, I would ask you to marry me."

She smiled, and ten years fell from her face.

"You just made my day, and, by the way, you are not so small. Just sayin'."

"Now, you've made my day. Thanks, Beatrice."

Max left a very generous tip, and Beatrice packed up the leftover pancakes and sausage in a to-go container.

As Max headed south toward Arkansas, his days consisted of driving a few hundred miles, stopping as often as he saw civilization. We're talking over 50,000 square miles. Talk about a needle in a haystack. But, the beauty of his mission was to keep people in suspense about the whereabouts of this mystery boy. Max didn't exactly make up stuff whole cloth, but he sometimes used "poetic license." So, sometimes, the boy was spotted with a wolf. Another time, there were some hunters near the Missouri border who swore they saw a tall, thin, blond male walking with a bear! They couldn't tell how old the boy/man was because he seemed to melt into the tangle of trees and roots.

Max kept stopping and talking and filming vignettes with colorful characters.

After the first week, he called into the office and was surprised when the boss himself got on the phone.

"Max, you son-of-a-bitch, you have struck a vein of gold."

"I...Is that good?" he asked tentatively. Never a good idea to assume with the volatile editor.

"Good? Hell, the first week of us running your reports, circulation is up 18%! And, from the many calls we are getting, they are starving for more of your reports."

"But boss, I don't think I'm much closer to finding this ghost than when I first started."

"That doesn't matter. Don't you see? People have bought into the whole mystery boy theory, and the way you describe things, they feel they are right there with you. Max, I think you have found your niche. Keep up the good work. Might be a raise in it for you when you get back. Oh, and Doris says she misses you, whatever that means."

"OK boss. I'll get back on the road and see where it takes me."

Max smiled. 'Maybe, it wasn't just the hat.'

He decided to head along the Merrimac River, figuring that the boy might want to be around a body of water where there were fish. Hey, it was just a guess, but this whole thing is a guess. Why not head down and see what the Old Mines are all about? It was quite a trip, and Max had to settle in for the night at a little Mom and Pop 12-bungalow setup. He pulled up to one of the bungalows that served as an office. Max walked in, and sure enough, there was an old man and an equally old woman. He was reading the newspaper, and she was knitting while chewing on something.

"Hello," Max said by way of getting their attention. The man lowered his newspaper and looked up over rimless glasses that were perched on the tip of a pointy nose.

"Hi there. Didn't hear you come in. What can I do for you?"

"Well, I'd like some lodging for the night."

"$20 a night. In advance."

Max offered his credit card.

"Do you have cash? I'd rather have cash," the man said.

"I can assure you, the card is good."

"Still..." said the man stubbornly.

So Max fumbled with his wallet and slipped out a $20 bill.

That brought a smile to the washed-out blue eyes of the old man.

"Is there anyplace I can get some food?"

"We have a vending machine just over there."

"No. I mean real food."

"There is a diner about 12 miles up the road."

"Damn," muttered Max.

"The wife doesn't cotton to that kind of talk, mister."

"Sorry. I'm just hungry and a little tired. Been driving all day. Incidentally, you wouldn't have heard of a young boy who roams these parts, have you?"

"Jethro?"

"Jethro? Is that his name?"

"It is if you're talking about the young boy who supposedly talks to animals."

"Yes! Yes! That's him! Where can I find him?"

"From what I hear, he doesn't stay put in any one place for very long. Roams all over these mountains. Walks. Never rides, although some say they offered him rides."

Max was so excited, he almost forgot he was hungry. Almost. But the grumbles would not stop, so he decided to get back in the van and head for the diner. Maybe he'd get more info there.

He almost missed the man offering him a key.

"Bungalow 7, down at the end. Should be nice and quiet."

"How many visitors do you have?"

"Just you," he replied placidly.

Max left, and the old man resumed his newspaper reading. Before he did so, the old woman had her hand out, and he placed the bill in her hand without a word.

Max was excited. So the boy was real. Just where to find him was another matter, but he realized he had enough material for a couple of reports.

He was smiling when he walked into "Jake's."

That's what the flickering neon read over an old silver Airstream recreational vehicle that was retrofitted with six rotating stools covered in green leatherette that ran along a maple wood counter.

The other side saw a counter fastened to the wall for standees. Jake was a big fellow with tattoos anywhere there was skin, a lot of them naval. He apparently liked his food because he boasted a 56" waist, minimum. He wore a blue baseball cap backward. He appeared to be in his early 60s, with a big round face that had a deep scar running from his right cheek to his chin. He had a friendly smile and asked, "Kind of late for eating, isn't it?"

"Oh, I hope the grill isn't closed," Max said worriedly.

"The grill doesn't close 'till Jake closes," he said in a third-person-like manner.

"Well, is there a chance I can get a burger and maybe some fries?"

"Wouldn't you rather have a steak?"

"I...is that an option?"

"If Jake says it, it's so."

"Then, by all means, a steak, medium rare, and whatever you have for sides."

"You hungry?"

"Yes, haven't eaten all day. I'm searching for this boy who wanders the mountains."

"Jethro?"

"You know of him?" Max asked excitedly.

"Everybody in these parts has heard about Jethro, but nobody can say they actually saw him up close."

"Where was he sighted last? Do you know?"

"Some say they thought they saw him down in the Old Mines area. That's about 80 miles south of here."

"Thanks, Jake. That's great news."

"Really?"

"Yes, but if you don't mind, could you put that steak on while we talk?"

"Sure." He went to a refrigerator and pulled out a steak that could carpet a small table.

"Wow. That's a big steak," Max noted.

"You said you were hungry," Jake said cryptically.

"No, no. It's fine. Really," Max hastened to add.

Jake slapped, and I mean, slapped that steak on the grill, and it sizzled, which just stoked Max's appetite.

Jake then grabbed a handful of potato strips and dropped them into a cauldron of oil. He then came out with a huge bowl of green beans, which he had heated in a slab of butter. Max could feel his arteries snapping shut, but he didn't care. Jake then brought out a surprisingly fresh mixed greens salad. He offered a few varieties of salad dressings, all without talk.

That was fine with Max, who was starving now.

Jake flipped the steak. More sizzle, then he plopped it onto a huge platter to accommodate half a cow plus trimmings.

Jake slid the platter to Max and said, "Bon appétit," which sounded so incongruous coming from such a tough-looking guy like Jake.

Now, there is no question that when you are really hungry, the first bite of anything delicious is going to taste closed-eyes terrific—pizza, tacos, and steak.

Such was the case with this steak.

Max was oblivious to anything and anyone as he concentrated on that luscious bite of meat. And, after several chews, his eyes lit up in appreciation for it being as good as he thought it might be. Jake busied himself with a couple of other customers but kept an eye on his steak customer. He smiled a crooked smile of satisfaction when he saw the steak consume Max, rather than the other way around. But, despite the best of intentions, the stomach will hold just so much. Max was not a big man, so his stomach wasn't very big either. Halfway through the incredible steak, he came to the realization that if he took another bite, he would burst or get very sick. He looked at Jake in defeat.

The big man understood. "Hey, you gave it a good shot. I doubt if anybody, including me, could have downed that steak in one sitting."

"But Jake, it is so good! I want to eat more. I really do! I just…can't."

Jake took a liking to the little man and said, "Hey, I'll give you some French bread. You can make one hell of a steak sandwich with the leftovers."

"Oh man, that would be great. Thanks, Jake. Listen, I am on a quest to find that boy who supposedly roams these mountains and talks to animals."

"Jethro?"

"You are the second person that put a name to my quarry. Yet, nobody claims to have seen him close up."

"No. He keeps to himself. Hardly needs anything other than what he can get from the water or the woods. Berries, plants, and stuff."

"How old do you think he is?"

"Nobody knows, but I've been hearing stories about him for years. Some think he doesn't age. I don't know. It's like Bigfoot stuff, except a lot of people have seen the kid."

"Just not up close."

Max explained about his newspaper running a series on his quest and wondered if Jake would mind being videotaped.

"Here?"

"Yes."

"Now?"

"Yes. That a problem?"

"Well, I am not really dressed for..."

"No. No. You are exactly right just the way you are, Jake. Believe me, the women will love you."

"You blowin' smoke?"

"Jake, I never blow smoke to someone who could snap me like a twig."

"Ha!" Jake laughed. "That's a good one! You're all right, little man. Sure, let's do the interview."

"OK. I'll be right back. Have to get the camera out of the car."

Five minutes later, Max, now quite familiar with the process, snapped on the auxiliary light and started talking to Jake.

"Just talk naturally. Don't worry if I make a mistake or two. They will edit it when it gets to the newspaper."

So, over the course of 10 riveting minutes, Jake explained all he knew and heard about Jethro. Max was beside himself with satisfaction because Jake was such a colorful character and interspersed his remarks with some observations that readers would find fascinating.

Max wrapped up the interview, snapped off the light, and set the camera down on the counter.

"That was great, Jake. Would it be ok if I recorded your sign outside? You know, just to give it a feeling for the readers?"

"Yeah. That would be good. Might generate some business."

"Great! I see you wrapped up my leftover steak, and I appreciate that. What do I owe you?"

"On the house," Jake muttered.

"Wh...? No. No. that's not right. That meal would have set me back $30 at a steak house, and I'm sure it wouldn't have been half as good."

"Thanks for the compliment, but still, no charge."

"Why?"

"Because I like you. You cheered up what was a pretty dull evening."

"Still, at least let me leave a tip..."

"I'm the owner. Who are you leaving the tip with? As I said, forget it."

"But..."

"Remember the 'I could snap you like a twig?'"

Max blanched and muttered, "Oh. Yes. I understand."

Max then packed up his camera, grabbed his doggy bag, and said goodbye to Jake.

Chapter 3: Encounters in the Ozarks

A few months later, Max was to return to Jake's for, yes, another steak. And, again, Jake would not allow him to pay.

"You know that interview we did? Well, I guess a bunch of people saw an article in the newspaper, and some say they saw me on TV in some news thing. Business got so busy I had to hire another short order cook and a waitress, and I still made twice as much money as I did last year. Max, my good man, your money is no good here, nor will it ever be. Thanks, pardner."

Max had gotten several segments out of the "Jake" encounter. And the people back in Grand Rapids apparently were eating it up and eager for more. It seemed that each colorful character Max came across was almost as important as finding Jethro. About that, Max was trying to understand how Jethro could have been spotted in such different places in a short period of time. He knew that people's minds and memories were not terribly reliable when it came to time and location. Any prosecutor worth his salt knew he could confuse a witness about what they thought they saw. But Jethro supposedly was spotted at The Mines one day and over 250 miles west to the Gasconade River a day later.

Max's stop at the Old Mines was a revelation. He had no idea that this region was one of the biggest producers of lead in the world. The mines had been going for over a half-century and showed no signs of drying up. It was hard work, but it provided jobs for thousands of people.

As Max ventured further south, the incidents of people having seen Jethro grew more numerous. He had a hunch that he might find him in Arkansas. He just thought the M.O. of the elusive Jethro fit in with the descriptions of people who claimed they saw a tall, thin boy with blue overalls. The climate of Arkansas was conducive to walking barefoot or with few clothes. Although one report was a little farfetched. It claimed that during a particularly harsh winter, Jethro was seen curled up in the arms of a grizzly bear, sleeping warm as a baby. Max was careful to couch the story as possible hearsay. But, it didn't seem to matter to the readers of the Gazette, who were now feeding other papers as well as local TV stations that were eager for the colorful reports that sounded like Zane Grey. Max used all of his creative juices in choosing exactly the right words to describe any incident. But, he always made it a point to end on a suspenseful note, much like a cliffhanger at the end of a TV season. The boss was ecstatic, which was somewhat of a miracle.

"Max, you genius! How the hell are you? Do you need anything? Anything at all?"

"N...no, boss. I'm doing ok. I know it's been over three months since I started searching for Jethro, but..."

"Hold it! Are you apologizing for providing this paper with the best copy it has seen in years?"

"Well, I thought I would be..."

He was cut off again by the blustering voice of his boss.

"Listen, Max, I don't care if it takes you a year to find this kid, if he even exists. Don't you understand? You have thousands of people hanging on to your every word, and they are chomping at the bit to learn about the latest episodes. And, I got to say, I never knew you could write so...colorfully. Max, you may have to think about writing a screenplay for the movie somebody will want to make about your journey. Max, you have struck a vein of gold. You need to work it for all it's worth."

"Thanks, boss. I appreciate the kind words."

"So, is there anything you need?"

"Well, this TV camera is really heavy and bulky, and..."

"Say no more! I have just heard of a smaller unit that is much lighter, has better lens quality where you don't need auxiliary light, and the audio is fantastic."

"Really? Boy, that would be a great help. The light sometimes causes people to squint and makes them nervous. To be able to just record them like a regular conversation would be such an improvement."

"OK. Where will you be stopping so we can ship the camera?"

"Well, I'm thinking that I need to spend some time in Arkansas. When I find a place where I will be staying for a while, I'll call in the address."

"You do that, Max. You do that. And, Max, I see you are eating like, one meal a day. What the hell is that all about?"

"Well, I didn't want to..."

"That stops right now! Screw the expense account! I want you to eat well and stay healthy. Understand? None of those nachos and burgers. You stop every day and have a good hearty meal. That is an order!"

"Gee, boss, I never thought you cared so much about me."

"Now, let's not get sappy. I want you healthy so you can do a good job. That's it. Bye."

Sure enough, when Max pulled into the Radisson in Eureka, Arkansas, there was a package waiting for him. It was smaller than Max thought it would be, but when he unboxed it, he was surprised at how the lens was of such good quality that it needed no additional light for good quality video. Max was thrilled with how lightweight it was compared to the monster he was hauling around. Max was anxious to take it out for a test drive. But first, following the boss's orders, he washed up and went down to the dining area.

There he found a brightly lit room with colorful white tablecloths on eight round tables. Each had green linen napkins and a candle in the middle of each table. Max sat himself down at one of the side tables and put his hat on a chair. He smoothed down his hair as best he could, but soon, a very pretty waitress, perhaps in her mid-20s, came over and said, "Hi. I'm Priscilla, and I will be your server tonight. What can I get you?"

Her smile was wide and genuine and lit up her pretty face, framed with blond hair fashioned into a ponytail, which made her look like a teenager. But her figure was anything but adolescent. About 5'8", she was full-figured at around 135 pounds. Max realized how long he had been away from females when he fantasized about those long, shapely legs wrapped around him.

"Ahem," Max heard.

"Oh. I'm sorry. My mind wandered there for a minute. Sorry."

"I was just asking what I could get you?"

"Yes. Yes. Uh… do you have steak?"

"Yes, we do. We have a wonderful rib-eye that is hand-rubbed by our chef's own recipe. It is very good."

"I'll take that, medium rare."

"Sides include mashed or French fries, broccoli, or peas and carrots."

"I'll take as many mashed potatoes as you can fit on a plate and peas and carrots, thank you."

"Great. Can I get you something to drink?"

"Would you have any beer on tap?"

"Yes. Several."

"Tell you what, Priscilla, you pick one. I'm sure it will be fine."

"Coming right up," she said cheerily.

Max watched her sashay back to the kitchen, and he certainly approved of her walking gracefully, but with enough hip movement to appear provocative to a sex-starved person like Max. However, as soon as he took his first sip of that cold beer, Max smiled broadly.

"You should do that more often."

Max was startled to look up at Priscilla.

"What?"

"You have a nice smile. You should do it more often."

"Well, that is awful nice of you. Tell you the truth, there hasn't been too much to smile about."

He then went on to describe his mission.

The waitress was fascinated. So much so that the chef had to ring the bell, signaling his order was ready.

"So sorry," she said as she dashed to the kitchen.

She brought back a huge platter with a slab of rib-eye that might have weighed at least 16 ounces. There was a mountain of mashed potatoes with a pat of butter nestled in the top of the potatoes. She placed a separate dish of peas and carrots, as well as a basket of warm rolls in a wicker basket covered with a white cloth.

"We have some great clover honey that goes great with those rolls."

"Priscilla, you are a dream. Not only are you beautiful, but you are thoughtful and kind. A rare combination."

The woman was visibly struck by the elaborate, almost poetic, praise. She was not looking to get that kind of consideration from the denizens of Eureka, Arkansas, with a population under 2,000 in an area of 9 square miles.

The blush on her peaches-and-cream complexion just heightened her beauty.

"I... I don't know what to say," she whispered.

"There is nothing to say. Just be grateful for the fact that there is one person in this place who thinks you are extraordinary."

"You speak... funny," she said.

"Funny?"

"No. No. I didn't mean funny ha ha. Just the way you use words."

"Well, I am a journalist, and that is my stock in trade. Without the proper words, you can't hope for a proper result."

"See? Right there. You just uttered some words that could be carved in granite; they are so wise. And... and... they just roll off your tongue like water off a cliff. Amazing," she muttered.

"Not so amazing. After all, I went to college to be a journalist, and if you are not good with words, you are pretty much finished before you start. It's not rocket science, believe me."

"I do. Believe you, I mean. I just wish I could speak like that."

"But, you speak very well, Priscilla. My God, if you had any more attributes, no one would even dare to approach you."

Another blush. "You are a sweet man, Max Longfellow."

"Oh, you know my last name?"

"Yes. I looked it up in the ledger."

"Why?"

"Why?"

"Yes, why would you look me up?"

"I... I don't know. You looked... different from the local men."

"Oh?"

"Maybe it is the hat or the way you walk or something."

"Well, Priscilla, I am going to make this place my headquarters for a while. I intend to go out each day in a different direction to see if I can get a whiff of where my phantom boy might be. But, I will be returning here each evening. I would hope I would have the pleasure of your company. You know, when I am dining."

"Only when you are dining?"

"Pardon?"

"I don't work here 24 hours a day. Maybe we could get together and... talk. I love to hear you speak. That is, if your wife or girlfriend wouldn't mind."

Max issued a small laugh and said, "So far, I am free of all such restraints."

That caused the biggest smile from the woman, thus far.

"Then, maybe, we could get together. You know, for walks and such."

"Actually, you know this area better than I do. Do you think you might take me to some places I have mapped out?"

"Oh, sure! That would be great! I have some time off coming to me, and we could cover quite a good chunk of Eureka and areas close by."

"Oh, I wouldn't want you to give up your free time to..."

"But, I want to! Really. You are the most exciting thing to happen to this little place in a long time. If I can be a small part of it, I would consider that an honor."

"Well, with that beautiful face of yours, the guys back home are going to eat their hearts out."

"What do you mean?"

"Priscilla, I videotape interesting people along my journey. And you are one of the most interesting ones I have come across so far. Plus, you are a knock-out."

"Oh, you are just saying that," she blushed.

"My dear, I speak the truth as much as possible. And, truly, you are a gem, and I can't wait to tape you."

"What?" she cried.

"Uh... did I say something wrong?"

"I thought you said you wanted to rape me," she said with alarm.

"Oh my God, no! I said I want to TAPE you. Video tape. That kind of thing. How could you think I would say, you know, the other thing?"

"I'm sorry, Max. Really. Men have always tried to get me into bed with them. Because I look the way I look, they think that I am easy. But, I am not. I am a good Christian woman."

"I have no doubt, and I fully respect that," Max said firmly.

"Priscilla, if this is going to work, you must trust me that I will not make advances on you. This is business. Incidentally, since you will be a business expense, I will pay you $10 a day to work with me."

"Oh, that is not necessary. I will be glad to..."

"No. I insist. You may have to lug some equipment and some other stuff. It's $10 or no deal."

She smiled and said, "Then, it's a deal."

The next morning, Max showed up for breakfast, and Priscilla was there with a bright smile. He thought, 'Damn! This is a great way to start a day!'

"Good morning, Max. I have some coffee set up at your table. What would you like for breakfast?"

"What would you suggest, hon?" Max said off-handedly as he sat down. He was surprised when he looked up at Priscilla, who had a confused look on her beautiful face.

"What is it?"

"You called me 'hon.'"

"Oh, I am sorry. I didn't mean anything by it, it's just..."

"No. I like it. It is sweet. I just didn't expect it."

"Priscilla, trust me, sometimes I don't know what's going to come out of me."

"No apologies, Max. You are a good man, and I trust you."

'Oh great! We are in the 'friends' game. Oh well, she is still great to look at,' Max thought.

As he was sipping his coffee, Priscilla brought him a platter of eggs over easy, home fries, sausage, and grits with several slices of buttered toast.

"Wow! This will set me up for the rest of the day," Max said gleefully.

"Well, we will be gone for a while, and a man needs his nourishment."

"No argument there. Thank you, Priscilla. Won't you join me?"

"No. That is not permitted. But, I will be ready to go as soon as you are finished. But, please don't hurry. Take your time. Is there anything else you need?"

The question begged for so many answers, but Max settled for himself thinking, 'A kiss from you would make my day.' Instead, he said, "Nope. I have everything I need right here."

Back in Grand Rapids, the newsroom was a constant buzz about Max's latest exploits. All of them were caught up in the frenzy of the search for Jethro, the phantom boy. The always-hard-to-please publisher of late had a big smile on his face as he watched his subscription numbers go up along with increased ad sales.

"Damn, I wish

I would have cut Max loose before this. He is a one-man band. He writes brilliantly, and the video, from which we get many of our still pictures, is like Norman Rockwell. He is quite a boy," he thought to himself.

One person who was not so happy was his daughter. That last night before Max left on his quest left an indelible mark on her. She had always been a little on the cold, some would say, frigid, side. But, that night, Max melted her reserves for the first time, and she felt, for the first time, unbridled sex. And she liked it. She liked it a lot and missed it.

"Daddy, when are you going to bring Max back?"

"Sweetheart, he has only been gone four months. The Ozarks take in a lot of territory. And, it's not like he knows where to look for this kid. I mean, he gets snatches of information about him being in Oklahoma. Then the next day, he supposedly is spotted in Missouri. Max has to chase down every sighting. That takes time. But, in the meantime, his series of the 'Search for the Phantom Child' is driving people crazy waiting for the next installment. I think this idea was the greatest one I ever had, if I don't mind saying so," he said with a big satisfied grin.

"Yes, but it is Max and his writing and his interviewing that is what has everyone in a tizzy."

"I'll grant you that. I always suspected he had a talent for the dramatic. I'm sorry it took me 12 years to realize that. But, when he comes back, things will be different."

"How so?"

"I'm going to make sure he has his own office and a byline. And, he will be able to report or write on anything he wishes. He has earned that."

"What about a raise?"

"A raise?"

"We sure couldn't live on what you are paying him."

"You still have a thing for him?"

"I always have. It's just that recently, I realize how much I miss him. We left off on uncertain terms, but I think he is the man for me."

"Well, sweetheart, you picked a winner. He has single-handedly turned this paper's fortunes around to where we are well into the black. And, my salespeople say we need to raise our advertising rates because there is such a demand for Max's reporting. The stills we are able to take from his videos have been great, and we feed some of the video to local TV stations that are always begging for more. Who knows? This thing could go national. Wouldn't that be something?" he gloated.

"I still want him back. Now," she pouted.

"Sweetheart, you are the love of my life, and I have given you everything you ever asked for. But, this is where I have to put my foot down for the first time in a very long time. The Grand Rapids Gazette means something again. I am not about to do anything that will detract from that. No, sir. I can't. I won't!"

The daughter burst into tears and dashed out of the office.

'Too bad, my darling daughter. But a situation like this comes around once in a generation. I am going to ride this pony until it drops,' he thought.

Priscilla, although dressed in jeans and a flannel work shirt, lost none of her feminine appeal as Max saw her near the car after he finished breakfast, went to his room to wash the breakfast off, and set up the camera for the day.

'My God! Is it possible that she is even sexier in that work shirt? Damn, I must be horny as hell. But, I need to keep my cool. I don't want to queer this thing. Whatever it is.'

"Hi," he said cheerfully as he approached the van.

"Hi, yourself. Max, I am so anxious to get started."

"Speaking of that, where do you suggest we start?"

"There is a general store about two miles from here. A bunch of old codgers usually hang out there, playing dominoes and recalling old war stories."

"That sounds like a good place to start picking at some brains," Max said as he got into the van.

Priscilla climbed in athletically, snapped her seat belt, and was ready to go.

Max smiled at this unexpected turn of events that was going to make his search in this part of the Ozarks a lot more enjoyable than he thought.

"What's in the basket?"

"Oh, I made some sandwiches, and there are some cold drinks in the cooler. I thought we might get hungry along the way."

"Priscilla, you are a woman after my own heart. Bravo."

"Oh, it was nothing," she blushed, but was delighted with Max's approval.

He had not shaved for a week and now looked a little rakish, along with the Indiana Jones hat, which he only removed when he was indoors. Also, lugging that monster video machine in and out of different places and the increase in activity had seen Max put on a couple of pounds of muscle. He was amazed when he had gotten out of the shower this morning and looked at himself in the mirror.

'Wow. Look out, you magazine idols. There is a new sheriff in town.'

He even had a bit of a swagger, which went well with the hat and the scruffy look. Apparently, the look was not lost on Priscilla.

He saw her giving him the once-over.

"What?"

"Oh, nothing. I just think you look... dashing. Is that the correct word? I've been studying vocabulary."

"Why, you sweetheart. Yes, that is exactly the right word if you wanted to pay me an extravagant compliment, which I hardly deserve."

"Well, isn't it said that beauty is in the eye of the beholder?"

"Oh, we are having a battle of wits, are we?" Max laughed. "I love it! Keep it up. Although if you become any more attractive, there are going to be few men who will approach you."

"Does that include you?" she asked quietly.

"Yes, you know, since we have this arrangement," Max offered.

"The Platonic thing?"

"Whoa, there lassie! You have been cramming, and I'm not so sure I can keep up."

She was quiet for a few moments, gathering her thoughts. She then said, "I like you, Max."

"And, I like you, too," he said amiably.

"No. I really... like you," she repeated.

He stole a glance at her and saw that she was dead serious.

"Uh... just so I don't make a fool of myself, which would not be the first time, when you say 'like,' do you mean like... affection?"

"Yes," she replied simply.

"What kind of... affection?"

"The kind where I would like to kiss you. That kind."

There was no traffic on the gravel road they were on, and Max pulled to the side anyway. He put the van in neutral and faced Priscilla.

"Are you serious? About the kissing?"

"Yes. Does that make me a hussy?"

Max smiled and said, "First off, you are probably the only person in the western hemisphere to use that term, and it certainly does not apply to you. But, if you were serious, you know, about the kissing, I need to do that. Like, right now!"

That caused the biggest smile Max had seen so far, and he was blinded by the stupendous beauty of this woman who could easily pass for a goddess.

They unbuckled their seatbelts as if synchronized and fell into each other's arms. At first, the kiss was tentative, and Max scolded himself for his scruffy beard. However, that did not seem to diminish the pleasure Priscilla got in the exchange.

After the first tentative kiss, he apologized for the scruffiness.

"I like it. It kind of tickles," she said as she went in for a more meaningful one. This one was a toe-curler of the first order. Her full lips seemed designed just for this moment, and Max was transported like he had never been before. While he was not a ladies' man, he had his share of dates and make-out sessions. This was not going to be a make-out session, but it held all the promise of one at a more appropriate time.

When they both came up for air, Max whispered, "I didn't think lips could taste so sweet."

"Well, I have not had a lot of experience, you know, kissing men. As soon as we start kissing, they want to get me into bed. Why can't they simply enjoy the kissing?"

"My sweet, innocent Priscilla, men just are not built that way."

"What about you? Would you like to get me in bed?"

"Hey, I am not about to say anything that might queer this sweet arrangement we have. I would be perfectly satisfied with the kissing and the hugging if that is all you are prepared to give."

"But, would you like to get me in bed if you could?"

"Sweetheart, you are the embodiment of every man's fantasies. Of course, I would love to make mad, passionate love with you. It would be the highlight of my life, thus far."

She smiled coyly. "Good to know. Now, I think one last kiss, and we must be on our way."

"Yes, ma'am," Max said and happily obliged, thus creating a goofy smile that he wore all the way to the general store.

As Max gathered up his camera, he asked Priscilla to stand some twenty feet from the store.

"Sweetheart, I would like to videotape you. You know, to give some background about where we are and that sort of thing."

"Oh, I won't know what to say," she protested.

"Don't worry. I will guide you along and, trust me, I will never embarrass you."

"OK... I guess," she said, not terribly convinced.

"Tell you what. If we do the interview and you are not happy with it, I will scrap it. How about that?"

"OK, then. Where should I stand and what do I do with my hands?"

"Priscilla, trust me. When folks see you and hear your sweet voice, they won't be thinking about your hands. Ready?"

"I... guess," she muttered.

Max snapped on the camera, and the autofocus was superb. He was able to frame Priscilla from the waist up with the general store in the background. He asked her some questions about herself, how long she had lived in the area, and other easy stuff that put her at ease. Max was amazed at how absolutely gorgeous she looked in the camera.

'My God, the gang back home are going to be drooling over this,' he thought. Without turning off the camera, Max walked slowly toward the general store, kind of like a video verité. He cut the recording when he approached the three old men sitting on an old green park bench they had confiscated from somewhere. All three of them were whittling on a piece of wood. Their movements were slow and measured as they took tissue-thin slips of wood from the main piece. They all were white-haired and well into their 70s. They looked so much alike, Max thought they might be brothers. There was a slight murmuring that passed for conversation as they whittled and chewed tobacco.

It was only when Priscilla came into their field of vision that they stopped being in their seventies and all of a sudden remembered they were men.

"Priscilla Collins. I do declare, you get prettier every time I see you," said the tall, thin one on the end.

"Well, Mr. Jeb, you are looking pretty fit yourself," she smiled and said sweetly.

"Shucks, I'm nothing to look at."

"You ought to tell that to the widow Cranston. I see the way she looks at you at the meeting house."

"Aww, that's just hogwash," he said, but there was no conviction in his voice.

"Listen, my friend here would like to talk with you and videotape the conversation. He is looking for anybody who might know something about the boy who walks with animals."

"Jethro?" asked one of the other men, a little shorter but obviously from the same gene pool.

Max said, "Yes, I believe that's what they are calling him. Jethro. Have you seen or heard of him?"

"I heard tell of some folks who were hunting quail in the Gainey Woods, not far from here. They heard a rustling and said they saw what looked like a tall, fair-haired boy in blue overalls. He was walking along with a huge gray wolf, and he seemed to be talking to some deer who were cozying up to him. You know, like they knew what he was saying. The hunters said he was there one minute and then gone the next. They claimed it was weird."

"Why, weird?"

"They said that the whole section of the woods where he was got so quiet, you could have heard a pin drop."

"Quiet?" Max asked.

"That's what they said. Birds stopped singing and tweeting, and everything was... quiet. They said it was eerie. But, as soon as the boy was out of sight, things went back to normal."

"How far are the Gainey Woods from here?"

"Oh, I reckon just under a mile," said the third bench member.

"Well, Mr. Luke, we'll be thanking you. Now, if you don't mind, my friend here will videotape you all. You just relax and be natural. You all are fine-looking men, and the people back in Grand Rapids, Michigan are going to wonder who are those handsome dudes."

"Now, you just hush up that kind of prattle, missy. We've been to the wars, and we have been around."

One of the others said, "Yes, but it sure is nice to hear it coming from our sweet Priscilla."

"Sylvester, you always were a charmer," Priscilla praised.

"Aww, shucks…"

Max captured the entire exchange and thought it was perfect. A few interior shots of the general store with its variety of objects and merchandise, and Max and Priscilla bid farewell to the trio.

As he stashed the camera, Max said, "Priscilla, that was fantastic. You were perfect. This is going to blow their minds back home."

"So, I did… all right?" she asked innocently.

"Oh, you did a whole lot better than all right. As a matter of fact, you deserve a kiss for your efforts."

She smiled broadly and said, "That would suit me fine. I was just getting a hankering for one."

Max happily obliged, and as they set off for Gainey Woods, he realized that he had never been this happy before. Like, ever. He liked the feeling. A lot.

Chapter 4: The Quiet Charm of Priscilla

Max had little hope that Jethro would still be in the vicinity, but he and Priscilla parked the van, took the camera, and started walking into the dense foliage. Max was rolling the camera as they walked to give a realistic feeling to the episode. To his astonishment, not more than 60 feet away was... Jethro! He was kneeling over a deer who was on its side, an arrow sticking out of its ribs. Max stopped dead but kept filming. The boy seemed to be crying as he petted the head of the deer, which appeared to be mortally wounded. As Max took a step forward, he heard a growling.

There, very close to the boy, was the biggest gray wolf Max had ever seen. It was as large as a Shetland pony, with bared teeth and a growl that suggested if Max came one step closer to his master, there would be blood in Gainey Woods. Max respected the wishes of the animal and backed up a couple of paces. By the time he collected himself, the boy and the wolf were gone. Just... gone! And so was the deer!

"How the hell is that possible? Here one minute and gone the next, with a wounded deer, no less? He couldn't have carried that animal on his shoulders. Or could he?"

Max advanced to where the trio had been, and all that could be seen were several drops of blood. But, no sign of the boy or the wolf. He and Priscilla searched a wide area for an hour and could not come up with any sign that the boy or animal had been there.

"It's getting dark, Priscilla. I think we should head back to the car."

"It seems a shame. He was so close, and then... nothing."

"That's ok. This has been the best day so far. I now have proof that the boy exists. Wait 'till they see this back home," he boasted.

"This calls for a celebration. Is there any restaurant around here?"

"Well, there is Rosie's. She has some great chicken-fried steaks, hush puppies, and some great sides."

"Well, then, Rosie's it is. Let's go. Uh... will they let a scruffy guy like me in?"

Priscilla smiled and said, "You fit right in with the Eureka crowd."

Ten minutes later, they pulled up to a ramshackle kind of cabin made of logs.

Max thought, 'This brings a new meaning to rustic.'

But, as soon as they ducked inside, they discovered a warm, cozy atmosphere. Sawdust on the floor, a small bar that was barely six feet long. No stools, but a brass rail that ran along the bottom of the bar. There were just three tables, two of which were occupied by some hunters who had stashed their weapons, one of which was a bow. Max wondered if one of them was the one who wounded the deer.

After being greeted by Rosie, a red-faced five-by-five woman in her 60s who had tattoos all up both arms, and one suspected, other parts of her corpulent body, Max figured she tipped the scales at an easy 200 and would not dare get into a brawl with her.

"Priscilla! You sweet thing. Damned if you don't get prettier every time I see you," she barked out in a harsh voice that spoke of many cigarettes and chardonnay.

"Hello, Miss Rosie. This is my friend from back east. We've been looking for Jethro. Have you seen him?"

"Can't say as I have, mostly because I am stuck in this hole all day. But folks say that they got glimpses of the boy here and there. But, hard to pin down."

"I... Rosie, I am Max Longfellow. I work for a newspaper back home. I wonder if you would mind my videotaping you and your wonderful restaurant," Max said in his most persuasive voice.

"Well, aren't you a sweet bit of Yankee meat," she said salaciously.

Max felt his skin crawl at the thought of being in the sweaty clutches of this troll. But, he put on a smile and thanked her. "So, would it be all right?"

"Sure. I don't give a damn. First, let me get you folks something to eat. Be right back."

Max and Priscilla settled themselves at one of the tables, and Max asked if there was a menu.

"No," said Priscilla.

"No menu?" Max asked.

"People come here for chicken-fried steak. And that's what they get," Priscilla said matter-of-factly.

Within minutes, Rosie was there with two steins of beer in one hand and a platter containing two large dishes in the other.

"Here you go," she said as she ungraciously plopped the plates on the table.

Max was astounded. There was a sizzling chicken-fried steak on his plate with hush puppies and some okra.

"H... how was it possible for you to do this?" Max asked.

"It's what I do. Now, git to it while it's hot. We'll talk later."

Max took his first bite of the steak and was not at all prepared for what he tasted.

"Priscilla! This is fantastic!"

"You never had chicken-fried steak before?"

"No. Now, I think this is the only way to go," he said enthusiastically.

There was little conversation as Priscilla matched Max bite for bite. After all, she was a big woman. Beautiful, indeed, but big.

"I love these hush puppies, Priscilla. Do you know how to make these?"

"Everybody in Eureka knows how to make hush puppies. It's kind of a staple. Like grits."

When Max and Priscilla had slowed down, Rosie came over and pulled up a chair. But, instead of sitting like a normal person, she turned the back to the table and straddled the chair, her two chunky legs barely touching the floor.

'Thank God she is wearing jeans,' Max thought.

"So, I understand you are on the hunt for the Jethro boy," she said without preamble.

"Yes. My newspaper back in Grand Rapids has ordered me to try to find this boy who seems to be a ghost of some kind."

"Oh, he is no ghost. I can tell you that," Rosie said emphatically.

"Why do you say that?"

"Because too many people have gotten a glimpse of him, and they all describe him the same way. Tall, thin, blond, blue overalls, and... sad."

"Sad?"

"That's what the folks tell me. He always seems like he is carrying the weight of the world on his shoulders."

"How old do you think he is?" Max asked.

"Hard to say. Some say maybe 14. But he has shown up in places for some time now, so he could be older."

"Do you have any suggestion where we might look for him? We spotted him in Gainey Woods, but that big wolf wouldn't allow us to get close. But, I could swear that he saw us. As soon as we retreated a few steps, he was gone. Just... gone. And a wounded deer with him! How the heck could a boy carry a good-sized deer?"

"I'm afraid you are going to have more questions than answers. There is something... something..."

"Yes?"

"Supernatural about him. Do you notice the forest grows deathly quiet when he is spotted?"

"No. I didn't know that. No, wait a minute. I think you are right. There was that moment when our eyes met, and the whole world seemed to stop making a sound. Any sound. From bird or beast. As soon as he was out of sight, the normal sounds resumed."

"As I said, something supernatural about that boy," Rosie said philosophically.

"How long have you heard stories about Jethro?"

"Oh, must be going on 15 years now," Rosie said simply.

"Now, wait a minute! Are you telling me that this 14-year-old boy has been around for 15 years?" Max almost shrieked.

"Yep," Rosie said with maddening simplicity.

"I... I don't understand," Max said lamely.

"Nobody does, really. Some think his mother gave birth to several children."

"Does anyone know who the mother is?"

Rosie looked at him smartly and quipped, "Well, if we knew that, why, we would just go up and ask her, now wouldn't we?"

Max grinned and admitted it was a foolish statement.

"But Eureka is a small area," Max insisted.

"He is not limited to Eureka or even Arkansas. He's been spotted in Oklahoma and Missouri. Some say he was even spotted once in north Texas. But the kid has become like folklore. I get the feeling there are people who are secretly helping him," Rosie said.

"What makes you say that?" Max asked.

"Well, there was a story going around that a trapper came upon the boy kneeling next to a raccoon, whose head was in the boy's lap. He was comforting the dying animal when his eyes met those of the trapper. The spring on the trap was too much for the boy, but according to the trapper, the boy's eyes begged for help for the animal. When the trapper went to get a pry bar, the boy was gone, but he released the raccoon, which quickly limped into the woods. From that day forward, the trapper would not use that kind of trap, relying on a cage set up. He told friends it was his 'Come-to-Jesus moment,' and he was the better for it."

"Rosie, would you mind if I interviewed you? You have such a wealth of knowledge about this that the folks back home will find fascinating."

"Who would want to see an old hag like me on television and in the papers?"

"Oh, Rosie, you must know there is a lid for every pot. Besides, you are one of the most colorful characters I have come across yet. Please?"

"Well, I never could resist a handsome man. Sure. Why the hell not?"

Max wondered at the remark and thought about the hat again. 'Whatever,' he thought.

Max was so grateful that the new camera was so unobtrusive, required no auxiliary light, and was quiet as a mouse. Since they covered all of the ground they had previously discussed, the interview went extremely well. After 17 minutes, Max signed off and turned the camera off.

"Rosie, that was fabulous. You are a natural at this. Don't be surprised if some magazines don't come a-courtin.'"

"You are just jerking my chain," she protested.

"Rosie. Look at me," Max said seriously.

"What?" she said offhandedly.

"I said look at me. Closely."

She did and asked, "So?"

"You know people. I know that you know people. Do you think these are eyes that would lie to you?"

Obviously uncomfortable, the older woman muttered, "Well... no. I guess not."

Max wouldn't let her off that easy.

"Rosie...?"

"OK. I'm sure you wouldn't lie to me, but that doesn't mean what you say will happen."

"I said it could, and I wouldn't be a bit surprised."

As they left the restaurant, Max was ecstatic.

"Priscilla, we have enough material here for five episodes, at least. This has been a gold mine, thanks in large part to you. So, after I file my report tonight, you and I are going to take the day off."

"The day off?"

"Yes, we are going to do anything you want to do. No work. No talk of work. Nothing but you and me. How does that sound?"

"Oh, that sounds wonderful!" she cried. "I haven't had a real day off in ages. At least, not with someone like you."

"So, what would you like to do?" he asked.

"This may sound trite," she cautioned.

"That's my middle name. Spill it."

"I would like to pack a picnic lunch and go to this spot. It's on a lake, and there are some willow trees. It is so peaceful and quiet. We could spread a blanket and talk."

"Sounds great to me. Consider it a deal. But, I don't want you to go to the trouble of making the sandwiches. I'm sure there is a deli or someplace that does that."

"But... I want to do it," she said almost pathetically.

Max then discovered that when she batted those baby blues at him, he was gone.

"Whatever you want, sweetheart. Whatever you want," Max said with a big smile.

"Holy Smokes!" bellowed the huge publisher of the Grand Rapids Gazette. "Just when I thought this couldn't get any better, Max sends me interviews and commentary with this beautiful Arkansas beauty, who photographs like a million bucks. The guys are going to eat this up! Oh Max, you sweet son-of-a-bitch!"

"Daddy, what's got into you?"

"Doris, that man of yours just keeps getting better and better with every episode he sends us. This latest one involves his actually having seen Jethro. Uh... that's the name of the boy, and..."

"Daddy, I know all about the 'quest,' and all that. You didn't send me to Wellesley for nothing."

"Of course, sweetheart. I'm sorry. I get so excited. Actually, I haven't been this excited about anything in a long time. Your sainted mother the exception, of course. But the combination of Max's writing plus his interviews with truly interesting people has opened up a vein of interest we haven't seen for quite a while."

As luck would have it, Max decided to call into the office before going on the picnic with Priscilla.

"Hello, boss. How are things going?"

"Max! I was just raving about your latest reports. Those people are damn interesting. And, that beautiful blonde is not hard on the eyes, either."

"Aww, she is helping me out with the locals. Boss, I hope you don't mind, but I am paying her $10 a day. You know, to help set up interviews and stuff. I'll pay her out of my pocket if..."

"Don't even think of that," the boss said hurriedly. "Whatever you are doing is working, so don't rock the boat."

"So, what did you think of the shot of Jethro?" Max asked excitedly.

"What shot?"

"The shot. You know, with the wolf, the deer... the shot," Max said, frantically.

"Max, I know what you are talking about. I saw the deer, and that wolf looks like it could run in the derby. But, no Jethro."

"I don't understand," Max muttered. "I am sure I captured the shot. True, I didn't look at it before sending it off, but I know what I saw, boss."

"I have no doubt, son. Sometimes a glitch can occur. Maybe you'll get him next time. I don't want you stressing over this. I have enough stuff to run for two weeks. We are parceling this stuff out bit by bit. Let me tell you, Max. The readers and the media are eating it up. We just keep them dangling. It's delicious!"

"Still, I can't figure the Jethro thing," Max muttered.

"Forget it. Keep up the search and... great work, Max. Great work."

"What is it, Max?"

"Priscilla, remember us seeing Jethro and the wolf and the deer?"

"Of course. I can never forget that," she said with a shudder.

"Well, I just talked to my boss and he saw the deer and the wolf, but no Jethro."

"I... I don't understand," she said as she furrowed her pretty brow.

"Me, either. I was sure the boy was framed in the shot. I would swear to it," Max said with exasperation.

"Max, please try to forget it. At least, for today. We have our picnic. I made some ham and cheese on rye and..."

"How did you know that is my favorite sandwich in the whole world?"

"It is? I just took a guess. But, I'm glad. I also have some potato salad and pickles and some great donuts I picked up this morning at the bakery. Max, they were still warm. Of course, I have some beer as well as some soft drinks."

"I think you have covered it all," Max said with admiration.

"Then, can we forget everything? At least for today?" she pleaded.

"Of course, sweetheart. It is a beautiful day. Let's go and enjoy it."

"Oh, goody!" she squealed.

'Goody?' Max thought. 'Why the hell not? If someone is as gorgeous as she is, 'goody' is just fine.'

Since Priscilla was familiar with the ins and outs of the terrain leading to the lake, he allowed her to drive the van. He deliberately left the camera at the motel. This was an all-pleasure day, and he did not want any distractions from his wonderful Priscilla. He caught himself. "My Priscilla?" Could that actually be? He had dreamed of such a thing, but he could see no way to make it happen. Or, could he? 'OK, let's quit this daydreaming and get on with the pleasure at hand,' he decided. 'Let's see what the day will bring.'

Priscilla kept up a lively chatter on their drive. Max learned that she was an only child and that both her parents had died during the pandemic. She lived alone in one of the efficiency suites in the Radisson. She indicated that they gave her some kind of break on the rent since she was an employee. She did not know what the future would bring and was living day to day. She was as happy as was possible under the circumstances. The good part was that she was always surrounded by friends she worked with and, of course, friends her family had known before they passed. You could say she was at loose ends. But, she was smart, and what she may have lacked in book learning, she more than made up for it with common sense. She quickly picked up on Max's instructions and rarely had to ask a second time, although he encouraged her to ask about anything she was uncertain about.

"Here we are," she sang out in her lovely voice, as she expertly pulled the van off the gravel road and under the shade of a huge weeping willow that grew at the edge of a small but beautiful lake. A couple of white swans floated regally by like some beautiful float.

"Priscilla, this is... like, fantastic! It is so quiet and just... beautiful," he gasped.

"I am so glad you like it. It is one of my favorite spots where I come and think."

As he helped her get the basket and cooler out of the van, he asked, "What do you think about?"

"Oh, all kinds of things. Mostly nonsense, I'm sure, but that's what dreams are all about, aren't they?"

"Priscilla, that is kind of profound. Did you come up with that?"

"I don't know what you mean. It's just the way I feel."

"Well, I would like to hear more about these dreams of yours. But first, I am starving. I skipped breakfast, so I am ready for my sandwich."

"Your first sandwich," she corrected cutely.

"Oh ho! Now you really are a girl after my own heart. My motto is 'If one sandwich is good, two will be better.'"

"Oh Max, you are so funny," she said as she twittered.

'I am?' he thought. 'Beats me, but, hey, let's go with it.'

Priscilla spread a scotch plaid blanket on some grass under the willow and she set about putting plates and napkins in place. She had taken several large plastic cups from the hotel. She did not care to drink out of paper cups.

Max admired her sense of detail and neatness. Despite the fact they were on a picnic, she insisted on wearing a beautiful yellow dress that had blue violets sprayed across the wide hem that hit her at mid-calf. It fit her tiny waist perfectly, but it was hard-pressed to contain the more than ample breasts, which provided maddening cleavage for Max. She was an absolute dream and he could not believe he was here with her. He also had a revelation. This is where he would want to be above anyplace else. Her blond hair was caught up in a ponytail with a blue scrunchie. She wore no jewelry at all, except for some small golden hoop earrings.

Max could not resist commenting on how lovely she looked.

"I'm glad you approve. I wanted to look nice for you," she said so simply that Max had to catch his breath.

"Priscilla, you are the first woman who has ever said that to me, and I thank you. And, if you don't mind, I need to kiss you. Right now," he said urgently.

She smiled coyly and ducked her head and said, "Need?"

"Yes. It is urgent," he repeated.

"Well, I certainly don't want to keep you in pain."

She then leaned toward him, and he got a glimpse of those gorgeous breasts and soon felt them slightly as they joined for a rather chaste kiss.

When they parted after ten seconds, Max said, "Just so you know, that will do. For now."

She smirked and said, "We'll see."

The next hour was about as unlikely as Max could imagine. And, Max had a good imagination. Birds were singing, swans were swimming, and he had just consumed the best ham and cheese on rye he had ever had. Plus, he had the pleasure of the most beautiful woman he had ever seen.

'I can't believe I did anything to deserve this, but I will enjoy it to the hilt.' They talked of small things that made for pleasant conversation. Finally, Max stretched out on the blanket and looked up at the cotton ball clouds. With his hands behind his neck, he had a goofy grin on his face.

"What are you smiling at, Max?"

"Priscilla, before I started on this journey, I was at the lowest ebb of my life. Nothing felt right. Everything was stale and uninteresting. Then, I meet you, and I am now experiencing the happiest day of my life."

"Oh, aren't you exaggerating a bit?" she chided with a smile.

"Not at all. I can say, without a doubt, that this is as happy as I have ever been. And, I have you to thank for that."

"Me?"

"Yes, you, sweet little innocent. You have lit up my life, and I thank you for that."

"Do you mind if I join you?" she asked primly.

"Plenty of sky for everybody. C'mon down."

She then nestled on his shoulder, and the scent of her shampoo set his head to whirling. Just to have this beautiful person next to him, breathing the same air, was a marvel to him.

He instinctively brushed her hair and just seemed to pet her. Apparently, it relaxed her to the point where she moaned unconsciously in her pleasure.

"You know, if you want to doze off, I will not feel insulted," Max suggested.

She sighed, "Max, I could stay like this all day."

"We have no place we have to be. We have food and drink. And the most comfortable blanket I have ever laid on."

"You won't mind if I close my eyes? I don't want to sleep, but, with my eyes closed, I can sense all of this beauty better."

"That's fine, sweetheart. As long as I can feel you on my shoulder, the world can go to pieces, for all I care."

So, time seemed to stand still, and Max wasn't sure if he hadn't actually succumbed to the hypnotic sounds of water lapping at the shore and birds tweeting. Whatever, he sort of came to with a start. He sneaked a peek at Priscilla, and sure enough, she was breathing easily with a small smile on her beautiful face.

Suddenly, her long eyelashes fluttered, then opened those beautiful eyes.

"Oh, how pitiful is this. I actually did doze off. Sorry, Max."

"No apology necessary. Truth is, I grabbed a few Z's myself."

She was quiet for a few moments, then she asked in a small voice, "Max?"

"Hmmm?"

"I think I need that kiss now."

"Really?"

"Can you oblige?"

"I most certainly can," Max said eagerly.

Bodies rolled together in the most passionate kiss thus far. That led to a rather torrid make-out session that lasted a good half hour. Both broke by mutual consent, breathing heavily.

"Wow," Max said hoarsely. "Priscilla, you are some kind of woman."

"Was the kissing, you know, all right?" she asked in all innocence.

"The kissing was spectacular, and I must be honest. That body of yours just made the whole thing a fantasy for me."

He was surprised when she said a polite, "Thank you."

"You know, I believe we have another sandwich. Interested?"

"You bet. But, I hope there is some kissing left in the bag."

"Oh yes, 'for sure,'" she said gaily.

What followed was a delightful conversation, with Max telling Priscilla some of his many stories from his newspaper days. She had the most delightful laugh, which just encouraged Max to be more entertaining. The sun started going down, and Max and Priscilla watched it dip below the horizon in silence. Max turned to Priscilla and whispered her name softly. She fell into his arms, and while the passion was muted and sweeter, it was absolutely the best way to end what had been a perfect day. There was little conversation on the drive home, and Priscilla curled up close to Max as he drove. He had his right arm around her shoulders and drove with one hand. He was, indeed, the happiest of men.

"Priscilla, I want to thank you for a day I shall never forget," he said softly.

"Nor will I," she echoed. "Maybe, we can do it again."

"That would be great. See you in the morning, sweetheart," he said as he kissed her lightly on her lipstick-less lips.

That night, he had the most wonderful dreams, all with Priscilla as the centerpiece. He wondered if this is what love felt like. If so, what does he do about it?

'Man, I can't deal with this or I will never get any sleep.'

Chapter 5: Whispers in the Wilderness

The beauty of Priscilla was also being noted by someone a long way from Eureka, Arkansas.

"Daddy, you never said that Max had a helper."

"Doris, sweetheart, he needed someone to help with the equipment and help him meet some of the locals. It's strictly business."

"Did she have to be so pretty?" she pouted.

"Is she?" the father lied. "I hadn't noticed," he muttered.

"Daddy, you are a big, fat liar. I could see you drooling over those pictures, just like the rest of the crew in the office."

"Baby, you have to admit, she is something special."

The daughter, all five feet two of her, huffed out of the office.

"Women," the father breathed.

"Hey, boss. It seems a couple of the networks are interested in Max's story."

"What do you mean, Jackson?"

"I just got a call from NBC and CBS. They wonder if we could provide them with some material for their Sunday morning shows. Want to talk to them?"

"You have their numbers?"

"Of course, boss. Isn't that what you always say, 'Get their numbers!'"

"Yeah," the big man admitted with a small laugh.

"Hello. This is Stan Grubins of the Grand Rapids Gazette. I understand some of your people are interested in a series we have been running."

"Oh, yes, Mr. Grubins. Just a moment and I will connect you with Mr. Kolinowski."

Less than 10 seconds later, Grubins heard a very cultured voice say, "Jon Kolinowski here."

"Jon, this is Stan Grubins with the Grand Rapids Gazette. You folks interested in a series we're running?"

"Oh yes, indeed. We have had several glimpses of the quest for the Phantom Boy, and it is quite fascinating."

"What are you thinking about? You know, as far as content?"

"Whatever you can provide. Of course, your paper will get full credit for providing the material. And, of course, the usual stipend."

"Stipend?"

"Yes. We pay the usual fee of $10,000 for the permission to use your material."

"$10,000!" Stan almost choked.

Apparently, the representative thought there was haggling going on and said, "I guess we could make it $12,250 if we can get more than one episode."

"Oh, I can provide you with as many episodes as you like. And $12,250 is fine."

"Wonderful! I think this will be so edifying for our viewers. Everybody needs a little mystery in their lives, don't you think?"

"Yeah, for sure, and we have plenty of that. You understand that this quest is not finished yet? This boy is a bit of a phantom."

"Oh, how titillating!"

'Titillating?' Stan thought. 'Is this guy a little light in the sandals? Hell, what do I care as long as the checks clear.' The ebullient network executive said he was looking forward to the episodes as they concluded the call.

"Holy Shit! $12,250 a pop! That's more than we take in from a week's subscriptions." Stan Grubins was one happy man, and dreams of that boat he always wanted were becoming closer to a reality.

The day after an encounter like the one Max experienced with Priscilla could either be very awkward or a continuation of the over-the-moon feeling they left each other with when they said goodnight. Priscilla ended all speculation by greeting Max at his door with a big, hearty, full-bodied kiss. He was surprised but was not dumb enough to spend time trying to figure out how this incredible woman was in his arms. He gave as good as he got, and when they parted, with her arms still around his neck, Priscilla asked softly, "I hope you don't mind this. I just needed to kiss you."

"My God, Priscilla, never restrain those instincts. It was exactly what I dreamed would happen. But, that was a dream. This is real."

Max took her by the hand and led her into his room, and sat her down in the chair next to the desk.

"I...Is something...wrong?" she asked with concern.

"No. No. Not at all. It's just that I may be jumping the gun here. But, I spent all night thinking about this."

"Max, you are beginning to worry me," she said plaintively.

"So sorry, sweetheart. This is new territory for me, but I'm going to go out on a limb. The thing is...I think I love you. No. That's not right. I am head-over-heels in love with you. There, I said it."

She was quiet for the most agonizing five seconds of his life. Then, she cried.

"Oh...oh...uh...I...I...didn't mean to..." Max babbled incoherently.

Then, she smiled.

"Priscilla, you are driving me crazy here. Say something. Anything!"

"I love you, too. So much that it hurts," she confessed.

Max pulled her out of the chair and into his arms. He swirled her around a couple of times, much to her delight.

He kissed her a dozen times like some madman. When he calmed down, Max said, "Priscilla, I've never been in love. I wanted to. Many times. Thought I was, once. But it wasn't anything like this. Priscilla, I know we haven't known each other very long, but I want you to know that the love I feel will eventually lead to a proposal of marriage. I hope you are prepared for that."

"Mrs. Priscilla Longfellow. I love it. As far as I am concerned, it can't happen soon enough," she laughed.

"Oh my God, everything is moving so fast. First thing, I am going to get you a raise so you can quit this job, and we can spend as much time together as possible while we hunt for Jethro."

"Oh, Max, do you think I should?"

"Tell you what. Stay right there."

He then placed a call to the private line of Stan Grubins. He never did that before, but the boss had become very accommodating of late.

"Boss, this is Max."

"Max, my boy! How are you, son?"

"Boss, I'm going to put you on speaker. There is a woman here..."

"Priscilla?"

"Uh...yeah. How did you know?"

"Hey, I may be an old man, but I can appreciate beauty when I see it."

"Uh...well...ok. The thing is, things have taken a turn here."

"You are not sick, are you?"

"No, no. I am fine. Actually, better than I have ever felt in my life. And one of the reasons for that is Priscilla. Boss, I love her, and she loves me. Can you believe that? I mean, the part of her loving a jerk like me?"

"I can see that with no problem. Congratulations."

"But, here is the thing, boss. I want her with me full-time for wherever this hunt for Jethro takes us."

"So?"

"So, I need you to put her on the payroll at $40,000 a year."

He waited for an eruption from the volatile publisher. Instead, he heard a very calm, "Is that all you're worried about?"

"Uh...pretty much, boss."

"Well then, let's make it $50,000 so you will stay happy and do a good job."

"B...boss. Are you serious?"

"As serious as a heart attack. Send me her information, and I'll send her a signing bonus."

"I...I don't know what to say, boss, but if I was back there, you might be in danger of getting a kiss on the mouth."

"From you? Ugh. From her? Now, you're talking," the big man laughed.

Priscilla spoke up. "Mr. Grubins, it's Priscilla. If I ever get a chance to meet you, I'm going to hold you to that kiss."

"Little Missy, that will be something I will truly look forward to. Welcome to the team."

"Thank you so much, sir."

Max picked up the phone and took it off speaker. "Boss, I can't tell you what this means to me. Thanks so much."

"Just keep those reports coming, OK?"

"OK. Talk to you soon."

"Max, I don't believe it!"

"Priscilla, I'm not sure I believe what just happened, but you know what this means?"

"Uh...not really," she confessed.

"You are independent. You will be making $50,000 a year! I'm sure that's a bit more than what they pay you at the Radisson."

"Not even close. But Max, better than that, we will be together as you continue your hunt for Jethro. I was dreading those periods when you would have been gone and I would have been stuck here."

"That is true. I can't imagine that I will wake up every morning with you at my side. Well, uh...that is...you know...after we get married."

"We may be able to move up that arrangement. I'm not saying the wedding thing, because that would complicate things. But, I do see the possibility of waking up in the same bed with you until we tie the knot."

"Oh, wow! This just keeps getting better and better," Max cried. Little did he know it would get better but more complicated very shortly.

Max sent off all the pertinent information about Priscilla, and then they plotted the next foray into the Ozarks in search of Jethro. Priscilla packed enough clothing and gear to take them on a 400-mile swing through western Arkansas, where some of the more isolated parts of the Ozark mountains are located. They made their usual stops at general stores and church meetings, always trying to ferret out clues about the boy. But Max started picking up a strange vibe.

"Priscilla, am I crazy, or are these folks protective of Jethro?"

"I think you might be right, Max," she agreed.

"What do you think we should do?"

"Maybe we should tell them that we mean him no harm and that if we could bring his story to the people, he might be able to help more of his critters."

"Priscilla, that is genius! Yes, that's the tack we should take."

"But, Max, are you sure you can deliver on the promise?"

"What do you mean?"

"Well, the worst thing would be if Jethro believed in you, but others, like the folks at the newspaper, and others, went back on their promises. I mean, it has been known to happen."

"Mmm, I see what you mean. But, I promise you, if push comes to shove, I will scuttle the whole deal. I have a little savings stashed away, and I'm sure I can get a book deal when this is all over."

"And, I'm going to save most of my salary and combine it with yours. We'll be all right, Max. I know we will," she pleaded.

"You bet we will, sweetheart. As long as we are together, they can't beat us."

With that determination and new outlook, Max and Priscilla started a campaign that their only interest in finding Jethro was to see how they might be able to help with what he is trying to do, which obviously was to care for as many of his animal friends as he could. Luckily, the newspaper had an ample supply of episodes that they parceled out frugally to all interested parties, so Max was free to resort to this new tactic. For almost two weeks, there was nothing to encourage him that his plan was working. But then he came across Old Cecil. Or, at least, Priscilla did.

This was a man that could be 70 or 100. In essence, he was a hermit. He lived on roots, berries, and some vegetation, kind of like a modern-day John the Baptist without the locusts. He had a little lean-to that had no amenities. At all. And that's the way he liked it. His shack was next to a clean stream. He usually slept out in the open, except during rainstorms. Then, he would hole himself up in a corner of his shelter, such as it was, and...well, nobody knew. Some speculated that he went into a sort of hibernation. He only weighed about 100 pounds and was a skeleton of a man about 5 feet tall. Generations of mountain people speak of him never changing. He was almost as much of a mystery as Jethro.

Max was scouting out another section, and Priscilla came upon Old Cecil by accident one day when she thought she had discovered the body of an old man. Priscilla, all pure of heart, leaned over the man and took one of his bony hands. She started crying, and as she was drying her tears, she heard a crackling voice ask, "What in tarnation are you doing'?"

"Y...you...you are...alive!"

"Been that way for a long time," he cackled. His throat was dry, probably from not being used for extended periods of time.

"Can I help you up?" Priscilla offered.

There was the barest hint of a smile on the craggy face as he said, "That's the best offer I've had in nigh on 60 years." His voice was starting to take on the semblance of human speech. He reached for a small canteen, and Priscilla supported his bony neck as he took a sip. He looked into her blue eyes and said, "I thought I died and went to Heaven when I saw you."

"Oh, you..." she blushed. "What's your name?"

"Priscilla. Priscilla Collins. And yours?"

"Cecil."

"Just...Cecil?"

"Old Cecil."

"Well, that's a whole lot better," she joked.

"Seems to have been enough for folks around here," he countered.

"That's true. I'm sorry. I didn't mean to be impolite."

"Missy, I've known you for 12 seconds, and I already know you could not be impolite."

"Can I help you up?"

"Don't mind if you lend a hand. Old bones aren't what they used to be."

Priscilla helped the old man up and was surprised that he was able to move around in his space.

"I'm afraid I don't have much to offer by way of food or drink," he apologized.

"Oh, that is fine. I must say your voice has recovered from...you know...when I first found you."

"Well, it's not like I don't talk," he said a little indignantly.

"To...whom?"

"The critters. True, it's usually a little one-sided, but they seem to enjoy it."

"I hear that's what Jethro does—the talking to the animals, I mean."

The old man snapped his head around and asked, "What do you know about Jethro?"

"N...nothing. Really. My fiancé is looking for him for a story for his newspaper back in Grand Rapids, Michigan."

"Why?"

"Why...what?"

"Why would folks be interested in someone like Jethro?"

"You know Jethro?"

"Yes."

"Just...yes?"

"What else would you want me to say? Jethro is a private person. He prefers the company of his critters."

"But, he speaks with you."

"Yes. I guess sometimes he needs to hear the voice of a human."

"Would you mind telling me what you talk about?"

"Oh, Jethro is usually sad. There always seems to be some critter with a broken wing or foot or something. He sees how people throw their garbage everywhere."

"Yes, it's a shame," she agreed. "Cecil, does Jethro have a brother? Maybe a twin?"

"Why do you ask?" he snapped.

"Well, he seems to have been sighted in places quite a distance apart and over a long period. I was just wondering..."

"His momma gave birth to two boys about 15 years apart. She liked the name Jethro, so she named them both the same."

"Do they...look alike?"

"You would think they were twins if you saw them together. Of course, one is older than the other, but they are spitting images. 'Course, they both took to wearing those blue overalls. Seemed right practical."

"But, they both just...wander?"

"As far as I can figure," he answered placidly.

"Their momma...uh...mother. What happened to her?"

"Nobody really knows. Some say she is holed up in a shack high in the Ozarks. Even hunters don't try going there. Grizzlies, wild pigs, wolves— all kinds of critters you don't want to rile."

"Yet, she seems to...get along with them?" Priscilla exclaimed in amazement.

"Seems to."

"Have you ever seen her? The mother?"

A smile crossed his face.

"You have, haven't you, Cecil?" Priscilla cried.

"Once or twice," he said enigmatically.

"Cecil! You are not...!" Priscilla almost shouted.

"I'm not saying anything. I have spoken more words to you today than I have spoken in a year. But, you are a pure spirit and you have a good heart. Not too many of them around anymore."

"Well, aren't you the charmer," Priscilla praised.

"Used to be," he said cryptically.

"Cecil, do you think you could get word to Jethro that we mean no harm?"

"If Jethro doesn't want to be found, nobody will find him. Either one."

"Still...if you do come across him...either one...please tell them we want to help in whatever he is doing."

"Can't guarantee anything, but, we'll see," is all he would say.

Priscilla heard Max and the van and went out to meet him. As soon as he got out of the van, Priscilla rushed to tell him what she had discovered with Old Cecil.

"Gee, he sounds like some character. Where is he?"

"He is just over there under those trees. Come. He is so sweet."

Priscilla retraced her steps from just a few minutes before but could find no trace of the old man.

"Max, I swear. He was here. I talked to him."

"Take it easy, sweetheart. You know these mountain people can disappear in the blink of an eye. They seem to just melt into the background."

"Then, you believe me?" she asked pitifully. Max grabbed her and hugged her and said, "Of course, I believe you. There is no one in the world I trust more than you. No one."

"Thanks, Max. But, let's get to somewhere so I can tell you all the things Old Cecil told me."

"That's his name? Old Cecil?"

"Yes, and Max, he must be a hundred years old. He is just skin and bones, but he takes care of himself."

"Boy, he sounds like someone really worth interviewing. But, let's get something to eat, and you can tell me all about it."

When Priscilla told Max all that Cecil had shared, he was fascinated.

"Priscilla, this opens up a whole new angle to the story. Now, if we could just run into this...what's his name...?"

"Old Cecil."

"Old Cecil. Wow. That would be something. Do you have any idea where he might be?"

Priscilla waved her arm and said, "He could be anywhere. I think he is like the Jethros."

"Oh, so we are pluralizing him now?"

"Well, there are two of them, Cecil says, maybe 15 years apart. That's why they have been spotted on and off for so long in so many different places."

"This is really getting mysterious. Well, it always was mysterious. Now, I am getting a different vibe."

"What do you mean, Max?"

"I'm sensing...now I know this sounds crazy...but, I think these guys have a pact with Nature."

"A pact?"

"Well, not a formal one, like a treaty or something. Maybe a better word is an understanding. Maybe, they are like guardians of Nature. As such, they may be able to know what animals need, and they do what they can to provide that."

"Oh, that sounds so lovely. I think it is safe to say that we could use a whole lot more people like them," Priscilla said.

"Well, you have your Sierra Club and other environmental organizations trying to help out, but sometimes that whole thing gets political. These guys are the real deal, just on a smaller scale," Max said.

"What if...?"

"What if what, sweetheart?" Max asked.

"I kind of told Old Cecil to pass the word on to the Jethros that we mean no harm and want to help with what they're doing."

"And that was exactly the right thing to say. I really do want to help, Priscilla. I know I started out thinking this was a chance to prove my credentials as a journalist, and I still want to do that. But now... I'm not so sure."

"What do you mean?" Priscilla asked.

"I mean that this is now bigger than just a story. It's a cause. This might be a microcosm of what's happening all over the world, with people no longer taking the time to care for Mother Nature. 'She's always been here and always will be,' they say. To which I ask, 'Yes, but in what shape?'"

"All valid questions, Max, but I feel so helpless," she said.

"Hey, don't say that. What you learned today is going to set them on fire back home. Even though we can't produce Old Cecil, I'll make him into one unforgettable character."

And that's just what he did.

Chapter 6: The Phantom's Promise

"Old Cecil? I love it!" yelled Stan Grubins back in Grand Rapids. "Max, the way you're piecing these things together is something I think even Hemingway would admire."

"Well, thank you, boss. That is high praise coming from you," Max said, surprised.

"Yeah, I know I've been tough on you, but you've proven to be the best reporter I've ever worked with, and I've worked with some of the best."

"Are you sure Doris hasn't put you up to this?" Max quipped.

"God, no! Hell, she wants me to bring you back now."

"Uh... boss, does she not know about Priscilla?" Max asked cautiously.

"Max, let's just say that I do not bring up the subject."

"Well, you know best. But seriously, boss, this thing seems to be coming to a head. We've put out word to the Jethros that we are on their side, that we want to tell their story so that the animals they love so much might get the help they need."

"That is genius!" The big man practically exploded with enthusiasm.

"You think so?" Max asked, a little cautiously.

"Absolutely! I can see it now. 'The Grand Rapids Gazette spearheads drive to save animals.' Oh, it's too delicious! The network guys will eat this up."

"The network guys?" Max asked.

"I'll tell you all about it later. Suffice it to say that you are a very famous man back here in civilization, Max."

"I am?"

"Yes, I've been feeding several of the networks and some other affiliates some of your reports, and they're loving them. You'll find a sizeable bonus when this is all over. I promise."

"Boss, I must tell you, this is not about the money. This has now become a cause for me."

"Jesus! You keep coming up with these incredible new angles that just beg for readers to sympathize. A cause. I love it. I absolutely love it. Max, you have carte blanche to do whatever you think is necessary. If you need anything, just say the word, and I will have it there within 24 hours. Guaranteed."

"Thanks, boss. But right now, what we need is some more legwork and some luck. We're going to spread the word and hope it gets back to the Jethros."

"I love that. 'The Jethros.' You can't make up this stuff. Keep up the good work, and give Priscilla a hug for me."

"Will do, boss. Bye."

"Well, Priscilla, let's go spread some of the boss's money around," Max said happily.

For the next week, Max and Priscilla sowed some seeds in various parts of the Ozarks. Wherever they found anyone who had a sighting of the Jethros or even heard of one, they left a small donation that they hoped would get back to the Phantom Boys and help with their work. Max was careful to indicate that the money was only to help pay for possible medicines and food or whatever the animals might need. They expected nothing in return; they just wanted to be part of the cause. These donations were only in amounts around $50. Anything more than that, and Max worried that some might be tempted to keep the money for themselves, although that was unlikely. Most of these people were poor and had been poor all their lives. They got by with very little and didn't complain. However, when Max brought up the subject of the Jethros, a slight change came over the listener. Whether it was reverence or fear was hard to tell. But, to a person, no one had a bad word to say about the Phantom Duo. They were like a proud heritage of something good and pure.

Max didn't know exactly how it happened, but one day, he and Priscilla were making the rounds of some churches and meeting houses, even at some general stores, when they returned to the van, which had been parked at the edge of a local forest, and there, not 40 feet away, was Jethro! He was just standing there, his monster wolf at his side like an obedient puppy, simply watching Max and Priscilla. Max didn't know how to react. He was caught up in the mystery, and everything seemed to quiet down. The look on the boy's face was inscrutable— not exactly sad, nor filled with any expression. Perhaps curiosity. Then, Max's heart almost stopped when Jethro raised his hand and beckoned Max and Priscilla to come forward.

Max hesitated, and Jethro could sense that he was concerned about the giant wolf that seemed like it only needed a saddle to carry him around the forest. Jethro, sensing the fear, placed a hand on the head of the huge animal, and it immediately lay down at his feet. Max and Priscilla advanced slowly, not knowing exactly how to act. As they came to within 20 feet of Jethro, he turned and started walking into the forest, looking over his shoulder to invite the couple to follow him. They did, not closing the gap between them, but following in his footsteps.

That's when Max realized… the forest was quiet. Absolute silence. No birds, no insects. Nothing. It was eerie, to say the least. Then, the silence was broken by moans. Moans from some animal who was clearly in pain.

Jethro stopped near the biggest grizzly bear Max had ever seen. The bear seemed to be entangled in some stout vines, thrashing around, trying to get free. The more it struggled, the more the vines ensnared it. However, as soon as it saw Jethro, its moans settled into more of a sigh, as if it knew help was on the way. Jethro placed a hand on the bear's massive head, which dwarfed the boy by a factor of three. Then, in another surprise, Jethro beckoned Max to come forward.

Now, Max Longfellow was anything but a hero, but somehow, he sensed that the animal would not hurt him. He stepped forward slowly, and Jethro pointed to a vine that was tangled around the bear's foot. Max fell to his knees and started working at the vine, which was about two inches thick. He pushed and pulled to no avail. Then, like the good Boy Scout he was, he remembered his Swiss Army knife. He flicked it open and very carefully started cutting through the thick vine. After two minutes of strenuous sawing, Max gave a tug on the vine, and it released its grip on the bear's foot.

The bear immediately sprang up, and Max thought he was looking into the face of death. The beast must have been more than seven feet tall, and Max could smell its breath as it savored its newfound freedom. With a look to Jethro, who wore the barest trace of a smile, the bear ambled off into the wilderness.

Max stood up, not knowing how to proceed, so he just stood there.
Jethro then issued a small, "Thank you."
'He speaks!' Max thought.
"Jethro, may I speak with you?"
A soft, "Yes."
"We want to help you in your work with the animals."
"I know."

"You do? Oh, that is good. We have money that we want you to use to help the animals. You know, for medicines or food or whatever. But, I am a reporter for a newspaper and I have been searching for you for months and....."

"Why?"

"Uh...why?"

"Yes."

"Uh.....to be honest, my publisher thought it would make for a good story. You know, you are famous. There are people all around the world who are really interested in you."

"Why?"

"Well, first off, you are kind of a mystery. You know, you come and go and fade into the forest. People see you and then they don't. That triggers the curiosity of a lot of people."

"You?"

"Most of all, me. I started out on this journey because my life was stale and boring and didn't seem to be going anywhere. But, once I took on this mission, every day has been exciting, and I am more alive now than I ever thought I could be."

"You want to know what and how I do the things I do."

It was a statement, not a question. Max was encouraged by the sound of the boy's voice, which had a slightly southern accent. The blue overalls were exactly as described. But, Max could hardly believe the boy was 14, as he appeared.

"Do you mind if I ask you a question?"

The boy simply looked at him but didn't answer.

"How old are you?"

He blinked his blue eyes and said, "I don't know."

"Uh....you don't know?" Max asked.

"I don't remember much other than what I do," was the enigmatic reply.

"But, you are not, say.....14?"

The boy looked at him with a glimmer of a smile. "No."

"But, all the reports....." Max sputtered.

"Reports can be wrong," was the flat response.

"One last question," Max said, and he was sorry he did because he knew this person would hold him to no more questions after this one.

"Do you have a brother?"

"Yes."

The answer was said with finality. Max waited for Jethro to take the lead. The boy then indicated that Max should follow him.

He wanted to alert Priscilla, who had gone to the van for the camera, but Jethro would not wait, and Max could do nothing but follow five paces behind this tall, thin… Max could no longer consider him a boy, but his cheeks were just as smooth as a newborn. He moved with easy grace, not straining a muscle. Just, sort of, gliding along. Max noticed a few things. When Jethro walked, he made no noise, neither where he stepped nor in the surroundings. Everything grew quiet, as if a king was passing through. Yet, Max, smaller than Jethro, couldn't help stepping on sticks and leaves and such, making a bit of a racket in an otherwise tomb-like atmosphere. Max had the good sense not to ask where they were going, and it was clear Jethro was not offering any information. Max feared that Priscilla would never find them, so deep they were going into dense forestation, but he had no alternative but to follow the Phantom boy he had been looking for all these months.

But, soon, Jethro and Max came into a clearing. It was remarkable since it was devoid of any trees or bushes. It was a wide-open field, possibly 100 feet in diameter.

Max was shocked, and Jethro could tell.

"H…how were you able to clear this much land?" Max asked.

"I had help," was the cryptic reply.

"Help? But, there isn't anyone within miles of here."

"Them."

Jethro pointed to a gathering of bears, wild pigs, and several horses, all of whom were munching happily on feed of some kind.

"Jethro, I hope you know that I am trying to understand. I don't mean to be prying. It is in my nature to ask questions. Do you understand?"

"Yes." Just yes.

These maddening single-syllable answers were getting frustrating, but Max kept his cool and asked, "How?" Just, 'how.'

Jethro gave a small smile as he recognized Max's cryptic gambit.

"I ask them."

"You ask them to, say, clear some trees and….they do it?"

"Yes. Why are you surprised? They know I love them and feed them and protect them. In return, they help, when I ask."

Max shook his head and tried to get in the frame of mind necessary to understand this very fundamental and not-so-simple boy. Boy. Hard to believe this 'boy' is 14.

"Jethro, I know I asked you before, but could you tell me how old you are?"

"I don't know."

"You don't know? Do you not remember your mother and growing up?"

"No."

"Jethro, I am trying to understand, but these one-word answers don't do much by way of helping me to understand. Could you tell me more? Whatever you remember?"

For the first time, Max saw thought lines on the placid but pleasant face of Jethro.

"It seems I always….was. I can't remember not being like I am now."

"Do you have any idea how long this has been going on?"

Jethro knew that a simple 'no' would not satisfy Max, so he simply scrunched his narrow shoulders in the universal gesture for 'I don't know.'

"What about your brother?"

"What about him?"

"Where is he?"

"Wherever he needs to be."

"But, do you ever see him? Do you ever get together?"

"We are always together."

Max was getting aggravated at these answers that illuminated nothing. He had to adjust his reasoning along a totally different line. But that meant suspending rational thought and venturing into the field of... what? The paranormal? Max was getting the feeling that he was entering a twilight zone and had to accept some facts that were impossible.

"How can you afford to feed all these animals? All of them eat something different, yet they look as healthy as can be."

"The feed comes as needed," Jethro said simply.

"Comes? Like a delivery?"

Then, almost a genuine smile, as Jethro looked around the dense forest. The idea of a truck or even a cart getting through the thick underbrush was just short of comical.

'My God! Is he talking about Manna? Like Jesus gave the Israelites when they were fleeing the clutches of the Egyptian Pharaoh?'

The huge gray wolf that was resting at Jethro's feet suddenly stood up. That frightened Max.

"Be not afraid. Sheba just needs to stretch her legs from time to time."

Indeed, the wolf, which stood only a foot shorter than Max, looked like any other canine just waking up from a nap. Her large green-blue eyes spoke of intelligence. Max saw that the animal cozied up to Jethro, inviting a scratch or a pet, which Jethro promptly supplied.

"Sheba is my best friend. We have been together for... a long time."

"How long might that be?" Max asked.

Jethro looked at Max and said, "Time doesn't work that way here."

"Like what?"

"Months, years. It's all done."

Max was starting to think he was entering the realm of Zen, which he knew little about, but the few phrases he knew were very symbolic and not terribly clarifying.

"Jethro, are there any other spots like this? You know, where the animals just roam around together?"

"Yes."

"Where?"

"Where they are needed."

Max was losing a little patience with these short, non-informative answers. But he kept reminding himself that he was in the midst of something truly unusual, almost mystical.

"And you maintain them?"

"Yes."

"Did you ever think of doing something else? I mean, in addition to caring for the animals?"

Jethro looked at him quizzically. "What is more important than caring for my brothers and sisters?"

"How can I help?"

"Keep the people away."

"What?"

"People may mean well, but they can't help themselves. They pollute my rivers and streams. Their refuse is scattered, and some of my small friends have choked on it. Keep the people away." And, for the first time, Max heard the word, "Please."

It was a plea as well as a request.

"But Jethro, I have collected quite a bit of money for your cause."

"Many of the people of the Ozarks are very poor. They could use a clinic or some assistance to help them buy enough food and medicine. That would be a good use of the money."

That was the longest continuous discourse the enigmatic man/boy had uttered, so Max took it to heart.

"If that's the way you want it, that's the way it will be," Max promised.

"You can do this?"

"Well, yes. The folks back home only know what I tell them."

"But will they not expect to see... me?"

"Well, yes, but, for some reason, you didn't appear in the video I took. I got a great shot of Sheba, but you simply were not there."

A small smile.

"Don't tell me you can...?"

Another smile.

"If you do what you say you will do to help my people, I will make sure you will get a view of me."

"Oh, that would be spectacular!"

"Your friend is looking for you."

"Wh...what?"

"Do you not have a woman friend with you?"

"Yes, she went back to the van to get some equipment some time ago. I hope she is not lost."

"She is not. She knows this land well. But, you should go to her. She is worried."

"But, how will I find you again?"

"I will find you."

Max checked his watch, and in that split second, Jethro was gone. Gone. Simply... gone. No noise. No snapping of twigs. Nothing. The big wolf, too. No surprise there. I doubt if Jethro went anywhere that the huge animal did not go.

Max hurried back to where he thought he had left Priscilla. Ten frenzied minutes later, he saw her golden hair in the fading light.

"Priscilla!"

He shouted her name several times until she raised her head and spotted him. Then, it was like one of those old Hollywood movies, where the lovers spot each other across a field and they race toward each other in slow motion with music building and building until bodies clashed together in an embrace of love and relief.

"I thought I lost you," cried Priscilla, as she clung to Max.

In his turn, Max suddenly realized that he never wanted to be away from this lovely woman ever again.

Then, as one, they shouted, "I was talking with Jethro!"

"Wait. What? You were talking to Jethro?" Max cried. "I was talking to Jethro."

Priscilla said, "We talked about a lot of things. Well, actually, I asked questions and he..."

"He gave short answers. Very short answers. Right?"

"Right. How did you...?"

"Same with my Jethro."

"So, there are two of them?"

"Yes, Priscilla. That is the only answer to how there could have been sightings so far apart sometimes."

"But, why are they so close, now?"

"I don't know, but tomorrow, I hope to ask him. Either one of them."

"Are you sure he will be... somewhere?"

"Yes. I think I can find my way back to the clearing."

"Clearing?"

"Yes. There was a big section of the forest that had been cleared and a bunch..."

"...of different animals were roaming around," Priscilla picked up Max's train of thought.

"So, it is true. There are a number of these preserves," Max stated.

"I got the same impression," Priscilla agreed.

"But, Max, Jethro said he did not need the money. I asked where he was getting all of the feed and food necessary to feed a Noah's Ark."

"And he said that 'It will be provided,' didn't he?"

"Exactly! Max, what is going on here? I'm beginning to be afraid of what we have discovered."

"I don't think we have anything to fear, just so long as we suspend rational judgment to things that are not quite... natural."

"Natural?"

"Priscilla, we have to be prepared for some things that will not make sense from a scientific standpoint. And I believe we may be in for something really special."

"What makes you say that?"

"The two Jethros coming together. I think we may see a... merging."

"Merging?"

"Priscilla, I am just spit-balling here, but I get the feeling that every once in a while, the two Jethros come together for... I don't know what. But I know I want to be on hand to see it."

"Are you... sure?" Priscilla asked shakily.

"Priscilla, we have come this far. We must see this through. Jethro even said he will let me videotape him, just so I could convince the folks back home to leave him, or them, be. It gets a little confusing."

"But, didn't you try that and it didn't take?"

"Yes, and he alluded to that. Don't ask me how, but he was able to nullify the photographic process. But he said he would let me do it sometime."

"Max, the wolf."

"What about it?"

"Was it with him?"

"As close as another skin," Max replied.

"Was it... female?"

"Yes. Her name is Sheba. Why?"

"My Jethro had a wolf, too. A huge, gray wolf. The biggest I ever saw. But it was a male, named Simba."

Max scratched his head. "Priscilla, I think we need to get back to some civilization, have a good meal, and get some rest. I don't know how much more my brain can handle at this time."

"I agree. The sooner we get to someplace that's normal, the better," she said.

"But Priscilla, let us not forget that we two are witness to something truly incredible. An opportunity like this comes along maybe once in a millennium. As a journalist, I am bound to see it through."

"Max, there is a beautiful phrase in the Bible that I have always loved. It reads, 'Whither thou goest, I will go.' That's the way I feel about you."

Max grabbed and hugged this pure and beautiful woman and almost cried for the joy of having found such a jewel in, of all places, the mountains of the Ozarks. The entire ordeal of the past eight months was absolutely worth it for that fact alone.

Back at the Radisson, after each had showered and made love almost urgently, they ordered some dinner and were sitting in as few clothes as possible, munching on some fried chicken and French fries and sipping on some cheap wine that tasted fantastic. Max not only could not remember when he was so happy, he couldn't even imagine being this happy.

He suddenly grew serious.

"What is it, Max?" she asked with concern.

"I need to marry you. Now!"

"What?"

"I don't want to waste another minute not having you as my wife."

"But, Max, I am already pretty much that, am I not?"

"No. This would have been great for the Max Longfellow from Grand Rapids or Boca Raton, but not this Max Longfellow. I want you, once and for all, to be my wife, legally as well as emotionally. I know you wanted a nice big wedding, and I promise you that you will have all of that and more when this is all over. But for now, this moment, I need you as my wife. Am I a crazy nut job?"

Priscilla smiled her thousand-watt smile of pure joy, and agreed that, "Yes, but you are my crazy nut-job."

"Is there a parson or somebody that can tie the knot?"

"Max, this is the Ozarks. Practically every man is a parson or a preacher."

"Then, I suggest you get busy and line one up for bright and early tomorrow. Also, grab a witness or two."

"That won't be hard to do. There are so many wonderful ladies here at the Radisson who have been so good to me."

"Great! Now let's toast our plan with another belt of this three-dollar wine, which tastes pretty damn good!"

The next morning, Max called Stan Grubbins at the paper.

"Max, I was getting worried about you, son," bellowed the big, walrus of a man who seemed to have only two volumes: yelling and screaming. However, there was a genuine hint of concern in his voice.

"Boss, you had better sit down. I have some news that will blow your mind!"

"Oh, I love the sound of that." The big man fell into a chair as big as he was, and if it could speak, it would have groaned.

"So, shoot, Max."

"I not only saw Jethro but I spoke to him. Well, at least one of him."

"There are two?" cried the big man.

"Yes. One, probably 15 years older than the other, but from what I understand, you can't tell which is which."

"Damn! This is fascinating," Grubbins growled.

"Oh boss, it gets better. A lot better and stranger than The Twilight Zone."

"How so?"

Max then explained about the clearing, the animals, the feed, and food that seems to... materialize.

"Max, this sounds a lot like science fiction."

"Oh, it's way beyond that. Ray Bradbury on his best day could not come up with something like this. Boss, we are talking about bears, big ones, nuzzling next to a deer or a horse. It's like a... a..."

"Eden."

"Boss! How did you come up with exactly what I was thinking?"

"Hey, I have not always been a big old cantankerous son-of-a-bitch."

"Aww, you are not so bad," Max explained.

"You don't have to blow smoke up my skirt, Max. I'm a big boy."

"Well, anyway, boss. I truly believe this is the biggest story I will ever cover. I need to see it through."

"Of course you do. Why do you even have to say that?"

"Boss. I'm getting married today, and..."

"Congratulations! That's great, Max."

"Uh... thanks, boss, and believe me, if there was anyone I would want for a best man, it would be you."

The big guy was suddenly silent. He had been struck smack in his heart, and it was so unexpected that it left him breathless for a few moments.

"Boss, are you there?"

"Y... yeah. Yeah, I'm here, Max, and that was awfully nice. You know, what you said about my being your best man. But, you know Max, I heard where I could be the best man in absentia."

"What?"

"During the ceremony, put me on speakerphone, and it will be like I am there. I'll even rustle up a damn fine wedding ring. A real one."

"Oh, wow, boss, that is fantastic. But, there is one other thing."

"What is it? Name it, and it is done."

"Priscilla. If anything, you know, happens to me, I want you to make sure she is taken care of."

"Max, is this thing... dangerous?"

"I... I really don't know. This is all so new. We are going back for another meeting today and Jethro said I would be able to film him."

"My God in Heaven! We are actually going to see the 'Phantom Boy?'" Grubbins exploded.

"Yes, but boss, I'm not so sure it is going to end the way we thought."

"What do you mean?"

"Jethro is savvy enough to know that if we prove he is real, a swarm of people will come out here looking for him, or them. They don't want that. They want to be left alone to take care of their animals."

"And what about all the money we have raised? I hear it is close to a million dollars."

"He wants us to build some clinics and provide medicines for the children and people who need help. And, boss, most of these people are barely subsisting. The ground here isn't all that great, and a lot of people are going hungry."

"In this, the greatest nation on earth?" came the bellow from the outraged walrus. "No, sir! Not on my watch! No, sir! I will organize a food drive myself. Damn, we send billions to people in far-off lands. It's about time we did something for our folks."

"That would be great, boss. But, the proviso is that it be as unobtrusive as possible. I don't need an army of people traipsing through this region."

"I get you, Max. Leave it to me. I will handle this personally." Then in a softer tone, "But Max, I don't like this business of something possibly happening to you. I want you to promise to get out as soon as things get hairy. You understand?"

"I'll be careful, boss, but you never know what may happen."

"Max, I don't like the sound of that. If there is a chance you may... lose your life, then I say screw it all. Come on home and to hell with the story."

Max then said quietly, "I can't do that."

"Why the hell not?"

"Hemingway wouldn't have quit."

The older man was struck by those few words, and he knew he was talking to a true journalist.

All he could say was, "Max, be careful. Be very careful. I need both of you safe and sound when I throw you the greatest reception this town has ever seen. Got that?"

Max chuckled. "Yes, boss, I have it, and thanks."

Chapter 7: A Union of Promises

"Max, this is Parson Brown."

"You're kidding."

"What do you mean?"

"Priscilla. Pastor Brown? That is right out of a Christmas Carol."

"I... I don't understand. But, he was good enough to get us a marriage license from the courthouse. I told him we were in a bit of a rush."

"And, he is a legit parson?"

"Young fellow, if I am not, then half the couples in this part of the Ozarks are living in sin. And, I don't cotton to sin," said the stick-thin man in his 70s dressed all in black except for his white collar.

He had a few gray hairs left on a large scalp. His small nose had rimless glasses perched on the tip of it, and he held a black Bible or something official-looking in his hands.

"Shall we get on with this?" he asked in a pinched tone that held a slight note of impatience in it.

"Yes. Yes. Of course. Sorry. How do we do this?" Max asked.

"We don't do anything. I do. You just repeat the words after me when I tell you. Think you can do that?"

"Yes, Parson," Max said meekly.

"All right then. Let us proceed."

He then went on about how matrimony was not to be entered into lightly. That there were certain obligations each party takes on. If they are not willing to, this would be the time to call it off.

One look at the lovesick couple, and he knew there was no chance of that. A little more window dressing, then Max remembered. "The boss!"

"Uh... Parson Brown. I need to make a call."

"Now?"

"Right now. My best man is waiting."

The thin man looked at Priscilla as if to say, 'Are you sure you want to get hitched to this crazy man?'

But all he got for his inquiry was a placid smile from the soon-to-be wife of Maxwell S. Longfellow.

"Boss! Thank God I caught you. Are you still up for being my best man?"

"Damn straight! Got a two-carat ring right here. It's a beauty, if I do say so myself."

"Uh… boss, watch the language. The Parson is here."

"The parson? If you tell me his name is Brown, I will spit."

"I… I'm afraid that is exactly right."

"Well, I'll be a…"

"Boss! Language."

"Parson Brown, eh? Why not? It's like a fairytale anyway. So, let's get on with it."

And, they did. In a matter of ten minutes, Max was offering Priscilla his school ring.

"You know, just until I can get you the one the boss has."

"Oh, this will do just fine. Thank you, Max."

He said goodbye to Grubbins and thanked him. He pressed a fifty-dollar bill into the hand of the parson who thought it might have been a five, which would have been his going rate. When he saw that it was a fifty, he smiled broadly, revealing all six teeth he had in his mouth.

"Thank you, Mr. Longfellow. This will go a long way to help provide for the family. They have been eating close to the bone of late. Crops and all."

"Well, Parson, that's going to change."

"Really?"

"Yes, that loudmouth fellow on the phone is raising some money to help provide food and medicine for folks who are in need."

"That would be almost everybody," the old man said.

"And, how many people do you think that would be? You know, in this general area?"

"Oh, I reckon it would be maybe 300 or 400 people. Hard to tell. Some folks live in remote places. But, when word gets out that help is available, I am sure they will show up. These are proud people and not used to people doing for them. But, times are desperate for many, and they will have to put their pride on a shelf until they get back on their feet. Sometimes, all they need are some tools and seed, and they are willing to do the work. If they are strong enough. Many a good man has wasted away from malnutrition."

"Well, I say, first we fatten them up, then we put them to work," Max declared.

"Oh, I don't think you will find a fat one amongst any of them," the Parson corrected.

"There will be after I get through with them."

"Those are mighty big promises you are making, young fellow."

"But, I have a bunch of people behind me that will back me up. Just give me a few days and report back to me. But first, we have a date with the Jethros."

"You actually spoke to him?" the old man asked in amazement.

"Yes, we had a long talk. He is very nice. Shy, but nice."

"Well, don't that beat all. Folks around here have been hearing about Jethro for ages, and it takes a city boy to find him. Tarnation!"

Max figured that was as close to profanity as the thin man would allow himself.

"Ok, wife. Are you ready?"

"Yes, husband, I am. Now and always."

And off they went, but were in for a big surprise.

Doris Grubbins considered herself a woman scorned. She and Max had a relationship. Well, it was on again and off again, but there was that unforgettable night eight months ago that was an eye-opener for them both. For her, a formerly lukewarm interest in lovemaking suddenly hit her stride, opening up vistas of pleasure she never even knew existed. And then he is snatched away because of some silly story about some hillbilly phantom in the Ozarks. To say she was peeved would be putting it mildly. Each day, she grew more and more irritable as the need for a particular itch to be scratched was denied her. There were no shortages of one-night stands, and she did indulge in a few, but they proved unsatisfying. No. It was Max she wanted. And, it was Max she would have. That's the way it has been all of her 30 years. An only child who had the double gift of having killed her mother during childbirth so that she had the total attention of her grieving father all to herself. Whatever she wanted, he provided. Coming from a long line of newspapermen, Stan Grubbins made the most out of a failing newspaper, but he knew that the paper's days were numbered. At least, until "The Jethro Affair." Now it is an all-new ballgame, and the future looked bright for the Grand Rapids Gazette.

But Doris Grubbins was, well there is no better way to put it, a vindictive woman. She hatched a plan to get her man back, despite the reports that he had taken up with some blond trollop. All she had to do was get her man back to civilization, and if that meant an end to "The Jethro Affair," so be it. She had overheard her father speaking with some people from the networks and major publications who were anxiously awaiting the next report on what was happening in the Ozarks. She placed several strategic calls indicating where Jethro was. This caused a flurry of excitement as even some of the suits themselves hopped on the corporate jet and flew to the Ozarks to have a look for themselves. That proved catastrophic for Max and the paper, but she was so full of jealous rage, she could only smile.

"Priscilla, I could swear this is exactly where we met yesterday, yet there is nothing here. Not even the clearing. Where could they have gone and why? I thought we had a deal."

"Maybe, we can go to where I spoke to Jethro," Priscilla offered.

So, they trekked west a half-mile but came up with the same thing. Nothing. No clearing. No animals. Nothing. It was disheartening, and Max was close to tears.

"We were so close. So very close," he kept repeating.

"Please, sweetheart, don't beat yourself up. There must be a reason for this."

Just then, they saw a Lear jet buzz the area. Eureka was so far off the grid that they rarely ever heard a plane overhead.

"Priscilla, we need to get back to the van!"

"Why?"

"I have to make a call. A very important call."

"Boss, Max. Yeah, yeah, I'm fine. Boss, did you mention anything to the suits at the network about my meeting with Jethro?"

"Are you crazy? Why would I do something like that? That would kill the whole mystery. Why do you ask?"

"The Jethros are gone, boss. Gone. Not a trace of them, the animals, nothing. Gone. And, I just saw a Lear jet fly over this area. Coincidence? I think not."

"But... but, even if that was true, how would they know...?"

"Boss, we are dealing with forces here that I know nothing about, but I would not doubt for a minute that they had some sixth sense about things like this."

"My God, you don't think...?"

"What, boss?"

"Doris has been acting a little wild lately. You don't think she would sabotage this mission just to get you back?"

"Boss, does she not know I am married?"

"Doris is used to having things her way, and I am responsible for that. But, I didn't think she would go this far. She had to know what this story meant to me. For the first time in a very long time, some of the big whigs of the industry were paying attention to Stan Grubbins. Max, I'll get to the bottom of this and get back to you."

"Boss, if I have lost the trust of the Jethros, I don't know how long or even if I will be able to reestablish that trust."

"Well, I think one way is that we are prepared to launch 'Operation Ozarks.' That's what I am calling the relief effort. There is a convoy of three 18-wheelers heading your way. We thought Eureka was a good headquarters for the effort. What do you think?"

"That is fine. Yes, maybe the relief aid will get back to the Jethros that we mean what we say. I can't guarantee anything, but I will give it my best shot. Boss, we were so close. So close," he moaned.

"Easy, Max. Don't let this eat you up. You and Priscilla take charge of the distribution of the supplies we are sending. We even had a couple of Doctors Without Borders offer their help. You know, with inoculations and treating some cases of whatever ails some of these people."

"That is a stroke of genius, boss! That just might be what it takes to lure the Jethros back. Boss, this may take a while."

"Take whatever time you need. I'll try to mend some fences here and keep the suspense up for readers who have been living day-to-day wondering what happens next out there. I'm not about to let the story of a lifetime go without a fight, I guarantee you that!"

Doris was nowhere to be found for questioning, but then, Stan realized that his daughter would not hesitate to get what she wanted or deny any wrongdoing.

"What kind of a wretch have I raised?" he thought with deep regret. He made some exploratory calls to the networks and, in fact, it was true. Some were heading south.

"Son-of-a-bitch!" he muttered.

"Listen, this is Stan Grubbins. Yeah, of the Gazette. Listen carefully. I need you to get word to anyone who flew off to Arkansas to see the Jethros. They need to turn right around and get out of there. The Jethros have disappeared, and they won't be seen until they feel safe again. Do you understand?"

"OK, get that word out, pronto!"

Meanwhile, he had to find a most disobedient child.

"Easy there, want to pull that truck up over there. Thanks. That's great," Max said, temporarily getting his mind off the Jethros to supervise the distribution of the various supplies Grubbins had sent.

He enlisted the services of the good Parson, who in turn put out the call for able-bodied men and women to come and help spread this unexpected wealth. Within an hour, the Radisson was swarming with volunteers. Max had announced that there would be plenty for everybody, so don't worry. He could have saved his breath because these people saw a beam of light where there was darkness. Simple things like sugar, flour, cornmeal, molasses, even something as simple as matches. All were floating like manna from the trucks. Even the drivers got in the spirit, and there was much laughter as some of the ladies provided lemonade for all.

Finally, when the last truck was almost unloaded, Max called for all to assemble.

There were close to 300 people there and more arriving from all over.

"When was the last time you had a picnic?"

Everyone looked at each other and couldn't remember.

"Well, we're having one right now. This truck has hundreds of hot dogs and hamburgers, and I even think we have some corn. Anybody got a washtub? Well, fill it with water and get it to boiling, and you will have some of the sweetest corn you ever tasted. Of course, we will need some volunteers to shuck a few hundred ears." Hands went up from old and young alike as all got excited at this unexpected pleasure. One so simple to most of the world, but, for various reasons, this region did not participate in any kind of wealth growth.

"Max, this is beyond wonderful. I took the liberty of videotaping a lot of the excitement. I thought Mr. Grubbins and the folks back in Grand Rapids would like to see what their money was doing."

"Priscilla, you are a genius! This is perfect. Oh, this is so great!"

Several big grills were set up, and the charcoal was just right for the seemingly endless supply of hot dogs and hamburgers. There was a festive air where everyone pitched in to help those who were a little too weak to fend for themselves. The children went around with their boundless energy asking if they could get a lemonade or something for the aged. It was a frenzy of cooking, eating, laughing, and finally, a peace fell on the crowd as they all could say that they were as full as they could be. That is when Parson Brown called for their attention.

"I'm not going to spoil this wonderful occasion by giving a long sermon, but I would be derelict in my duty if I didn't ask you to bow your heads and give me a moment of silence as we praise the Lord for his generosity. Generosity that came through the agency of Mr. Maxwell Longfellow." There was a thunderous applause at Max's name. He humbly stood up and waved his arm. Then, everyone quieted down to where you could hear just the birds chirping.

"All together now...."

"Amen," echoed loud and clear.

There was visiting among neighbors who had not been seen in ages. Eventually, the evening was coming to an end, and without prompting, a cadre of young and old scoured the campground and picked up every bit of debris.

Max called for the attention of the crowd. "Folks, if a member of each family would come forward, we'll spread the leftovers. That is, if you are not sick of hot dogs and hamburgers."

There were shouts of "Never!" followed by more laughter.

Priscilla was getting it all down on videotape that would prove to be worth its weight in gold.

As the last remnants of the crowd dispersed to their homes, a very exhausted but delighted Max and Priscilla retired to their rooms at the Radisson.

Max flopped on the bed, totally spent, physically and emotionally.

Priscilla sat next to him, took his hand, and kissed it.

"What was that for?" he asked.

"Because I am married to the most wonderful man in the world. Max, did you see the looks on the faces of those wonderful people? You know what that look was. Hope. Hope, Max. Something they had not experienced for a long, long time. And, you helped bring it about. If you do nothing else with your life, and I know you are going to accomplish great things, you will always have this day. I wouldn't be surprised if they erect a statue of you and put it in the town square."

"Please, let us not go crazy. I could not have done it without you. I would not want to have done it without you, Priscilla. Let me take a shower and I want to take a look at the video you took."

"Mind if I join you? You know, to preserve water and all that?"

"God, but I love you and the way you think!"

Stan Grubbins was on a mission, and nothing, business or otherwise, would distract him from his goal: finding his daughter. He tried her usual haunts, boutiques, beauty parlors, the gym. 'Nah, not Doris. She doesn't like to sweat.' After coming up empty, he decided that she would have to come back to her apartment. An apartment she said she "absolutely needed for my self-worth," or whatever the hell that crap means,' he growled to himself.

So, he let himself into the apartment he rented for her. She insisted there be only one key.

'Fat chance of that. I'm paying two grand a month for the two-bedroom flat and I can't come and go as I please? In your dreams.'

He settled himself in one of the chairs that didn't look like a bean bag, took his cell, and made some calls. One was to Max.

"Max, I was wondering what the fallout from the suits getting wind of Jethro was so far."

"Well, boss, Priscilla had the presence of mind to videotape a lot of what went on here yesterday. Boss, I wish you could have seen the joy on the faces of these people who have known nothing but hard times. They must have blessed your name a dozen times as they celebrated."

"Celebrated?"

"Why, of course. After we unloaded the trucks, I threw them a picnic they will not soon forget. I hope you don't mind, but I put in a request for hot dogs, hamburgers, corn, that kind of thing. Boss, I don't know if they could remember a time when they could eat all they wanted and then take some home. It... it was a feeling I will never forget."

"Max, that was so smart and thoughtful of you. Of course, I don't mind. Spend what you need. There is more where that is coming from. Especially when you send me the video."

"The parson here has a head for organization, and he has taken on the job of assessing what families need and apportioning it appropriately. Boss, the energy these people have shown in the past 24 hours would make you smile. They are eager to help each other. They are already thinking of renovating an old building that could be used as a clinic. That would be such a boon to the old as well as the very young who need shots and stuff like that."

"That's great, Max. I have two more trucks coming. I collected a bunch of used furniture that Goodwill refused to take. Something about 'isolated pieces' not being acceptable. Anyway, I picked up a load of assorted lamps and desks, and chairs, and that kind of stuff for anybody who might want it."

"Boss, that was super thoughtful of you and will be such a welcome sight to these bare-boned homes of theirs. Thanks again."

"Don't thank me. I have never felt so alive as I have since we started this relief drive. Haven't slept better in years."

He didn't know if he would ever actually tell him, but Stan now felt a closeness to Max he didn't even have with his daughter. 'He is the son I never had,' he thought. 'Better late than never,' he thought.

'Gonna have to amend the will. Doris is going to be in for a shock,' he chuckled to himself.

Max and Priscilla set out for their renewed search of the Jethros. They decided reluctantly to go in two directions to increase their chances of coming across one of them.

"Listen, Priscilla. This is a high-pitched whistle. I want you to use it if you find something or if you are in any kind of danger. Any kind. Understand?"

"Max, I appreciate your concern. I really do. But, I am a big girl and I know these parts as well as anyone. I'll be fine. You take care of yourself, my sweet man."

With a quick kiss, they set off. Max did not know what he was looking for. It was more of a question of Jethro finding him. Jethro has remained, for the most part, hidden. Max believed that the occasional sightings were just enough to keep the mystery alive. He did not think the Jethros had any ulterior motives, like being seen as some sort of gods. It was just their way of preserving what they cherished most: the animals they felt were in their care. To some, it might have seemed a rather shallow life, but when someone has a mission, it doesn't seem that way. So, Max wandered about, hoping that Jethro would find him. Of course, there was the matter of reestablishing trust. That was tricky. The convoys and relief for their people were a first step. After all, it was Jethro who suggested the aid. Max dearly hoped that would carry some weight when and if they ever met again.

It happened suddenly. One moment, Max was checking the time, the next, Jethro was standing there not 15 feet away. And, of course, the big gray wolf was at his side.

Because the animal was female, Max deduced that this was 'his' Jethro. Max stood stock still and waited for Jethro to speak, if he was going to.

"You kept your word."

"Yes, Jethro, I did. And I intend to continue getting aid to your people."

"That is good. I have not seen them so happy in a long time. It makes my heart glad."

"Good. And, I want to apologize for any concern you had about outsiders coming here."

"I know it was not of your doing, but we needed to… move."

"But, how could you just up and take… no. It's none of my business how you do things. I realize I am in a different reality with you. I'm not exactly sure what you are, and again, it's none of my business, although I am curious as hell."

A small smile. "You speak much. But, you have a good heart. I will tell you as much as I can. There are things that I do that I don't understand how I can do them. The animals, for instance."

"What about the animals?"

"How is it that I know what they are thinking and feeling? How do they allow me to roam among them, never feeling threatened? Really, I never feel so protected as when I am among the most dangerous of them."

"Uh… Jethro, that story about you sleeping in the arms of a grizzly one cold winter. Is that true?"

"Ask him."

"Who... uh... wait... him? That big grizzly?" Max was looking at a 7-foot colossus of a bear standing tall.

"Just shut your mind to the noise of the world. He is listening."

"I... I don't think..." Max mumbled uncertainly.

"Try."

Max realized that he was in no danger, so, as best he could, he tried to make his mind a blank. He tried manfully, but after 30 seconds, he became agitated that he could not do it. But, with his eyes still closed, he felt a warm hand on his shoulder.

"Now, try," was all Jethro said.

All of a sudden, everything became clear and quiet. And, Max sensed the bear! How...? He didn't try to take it apart. It was a wonderful feeling. Like he was really a part of the universe.

The hand was removed and Jethro asked, "What did you learn?"

"I learned that our friend over there is hungry and he has a thing for cornbread. Cornbread? A bear?"

Jethro smiled. "It's a treat for him but sometimes hard to come by."

"I will see to it that there is a plentiful supply."

"That is kind of you and our friend thanks you."

"He already has, Jethro. Thank you for this experience. I will never forget it."

"Your partner. She is searching for me. Call her to us. Bring the camera."

"Yes. Yes. Right away."

Max had a whistle, as well as the one he gave Priscilla. He gave it a quick alert. In less than three minutes, Priscilla came running.

"Priscilla, Jethro wanted to say hello," Max said proudly.

"Mr. Jethro, this is an honor, sir," Priscilla said humbly.

He smiled. "All these years, you thought I was a boy. Now, you accord me the honors of an adult."

"Oh, you are much more than an adult. You are a symbol. A symbol of hope and goodness in a world that seems to have lost those values."

Jethro looked at Max. "This one has a pure heart."

"Jethro, no offense, but I could have told you that."

A bigger smile. "Touché" would have been appropriate but that was not in the wheelhouse of this... this... entity.

"If you have your camera, I will make a statement."

"Oh... sure. Of course. Just a minute," Max fumbled. Then Priscilla handed him the camera and said, "Steady, Max."

After setting the camera, he started rolling and said, "Anytime, Jethro."

"I want to extend my thanks to all who have relieved the stress and hunger of my people. I hope your generosity will not fail. Again, thank you. Now, maybe you would like to meet Sheba."

At the mention of her name, the giant wolf reared up and placed its forelegs on Jethro's shoulders, her huge head still a foot above his. Max could have screamed in delight. It was so perfect and encapsulated the oneness Jethro felt for his animals and they for him.

The wolf returned to all fours and Jethro said, "That will be enough for now."

"Of course. Yes. That was great. Thank you, Jethro."

Jethro looked at Priscilla and said, "He is an excitable one, isn't he?"

"Yes, he is, but he means well."

"If that were not the case, I would never have allowed him to find me."

Priscilla said, "Thank you," and turned to Max for a moment. When she looked up again, Jethro and the wolf were gone. Not just gone. Vanished. Just like that. No trace that they had ever even been there.

But, Priscilla did not spend time trying to figure it out. She was beyond that now.

Max checked to make sure he captured the images he thought he had and breathed a big sigh of relief when he saw the shots were crystal clear. Perfect.

"Priscilla, this is gold. If not a Nobel, at least a Pulitzer."

Both laughed in their mutual happiness.

After three hours of waiting that was anything but patient, Stan heard a key in the door.

"Finally!"

Doris came into the apartment and was surprised that the lights were on, and it took her a moment to bring her big father into view.

"Daddy! What are you doing here?" she cried, partly in alarm and partly in indignation that her privacy was violated.

"Sit down," he said in a menacing low tone.

"But..."

"I said, sit your ass down! Now!" the real Stan Grubbins demanded.

She complied and sat like a child waiting for... she didn't know what, but it was not good. She had never seen the rage in her father as she witnessed now, and she dreaded what was to come.

"Did you notify the networks about Max and Jethro?"

"What?"

"Just answer the question, and don't try to lie. I can read you like a book."

"I... I just wanted Max to come home," she started to sniffle.

"Can the tears. Your stupid jealousy and greediness almost destroyed the most worthwhile project I have ever been involved with. And you will pay."

"Pay?" she asked timidly.

A smile of irony from the father. "Actually, you will pay by not being able to pay for anything. Those credit cards of yours? Might as well tear them up. I have already stopped payment on all of them. You are now going to live on what you have. You will not be able to buy anything you don't pay for with that stash of cash I know you must have."

"But, Daddy..." she pleaded.

"Don't 'Daddy' me. It won't work. You are a conniving little brat, and from now on, you will be working in the mailroom."

"The mailroom? Oh, Daddy, that is so..."

"Demeaning? Maybe. But maybe it will teach you how it feels to work for a buck, for a change. The gravy train has pulled into reality station, sweetheart. And the first day you miss work, you'd better find a place to rest your head, because the locks will be changed on this apartment."

"Daddy, how can you be so... cold?"

"Because I finally decided that I was not doing you any favors, giving you anything and everything you wanted all those years. I felt a certain responsibility of being both mother and father to you. But, no more. Shape up or ship out. Do I make myself crystal clear?"

"Y...es," she murmured.

"I can't hear you."

"I said, yes. I understand."

"So, tomorrow you will report to the mailroom at 8:30 a.m. sharp. Got that?"

"8:30?" she gasped.

"You have a problem with that?" the father snapped.

"N...no. No. I have no problem with that. I will be there."

"Damn straight. I suggest you dig out some work clothes. It can get a little dusty in the mailroom."

With that little bit of advice, Stan Grubbins strode out of the apartment. When the door closed behind him, he had to lean against a wall.

"That was the toughest thing I ever had to do," he breathed. But then, he smiled. "It was a damn long time in coming."

Chapter 8: The Turning Point

When Max and Priscilla realized they were alone, they were not surprised. They were getting used to the sudden disappearance of Jethro. Well, no one actually gets used to such phenomena, but let's just say, it is not as shocking as it was at first.

"So, what now?" Priscilla asked.

"Now, we go back to the Radisson and process this latest bit of treasure. I am going to feed it to the folks a little at a time."

"Why?"

"A couple of reasons. I think getting it all at once could be so overwhelming that it becomes hard to handle. The other reason, and more importantly, is the mystery factor. We can milk this for weeks. I can see the copy now: 'Jethro search getting warmer and warmer.' Yes, we have a future best-seller here, for sure. But, plenty of time for that. We still need to fulfill our promises to Jethro."

"Yes, we do. And another thing, Max."

"Yes?"

"The other Jethro."

"Oh."

"Yes. Max, there must be a reason why they are both so close. I think we are in for another round of surprises."

"Priscilla, you have been right about so many things that I don't doubt what you say. But, right now, we have to play this day by day. So, let's get back to base and see what we can send to the good people of Grand Rapids and whoever might be dialed into this."

If Max could have been the proverbial fly on the wall of a couple of boardrooms, he would have been pleased to discover that the interest, indeed, was still high on the Jethro Mystery.

"I'm told we came this close to queering this entire deal," said CEO Edward Collingsworth of CBS. "Which lunkhead was it that decided it would be a good idea to buzz the Ozarks in a Lear jet?"

Of course, there were no answers. That was tacit admission that the problem was "taken care of." Translation: the person is walking out of the office with a cardboard box.

"Let's not have any more scares like that," warned the silver-haired, tall gentleman who was in his mid-60s. His deep, mellow voice spoke of someone who might have spent some time behind a microphone, and his handsome good looks probably gave the ladies a little something to make them flush. "What is the latest report? Anybody know?"

"Sir, we just received a call from the Grubbins fellow who says he may have some dynamite material. He hinted there might have been not only a sighting but a conversation with this Jethro person by some journalist named Max... something."

There was a slight rebuke in the tone of the CEO. "First lesson of journalism: Get the facts. All the facts. His name is Maxwell Longfellow, and I dare say he may easily wind up with a Pulitzer for his work. There definitely is a book here and a movie as well. Let us keep him in our sights. When this thing wraps up, I want to offer him a package he can't refuse. Do I make myself clear?"

A chorus of "Yes" and "Right, sir." And the meeting adjourned. He then called them all back.

"I had an idea. Phillips, you have been liaison with this Grubbins fellow?"

"Yes, sir, I have."

"I want you to float the idea of us flying this Maxwell chap here for a brief interview."

"OK, sir, but I get the impression everyone there is involved in this relief drive that has had a major effect on the people out there."

"So?"

"So, I don't know if he would want to tear himself away from his work."

"Tell him that there is a $50,000 check waiting for his fund if he makes the one-day trip. All expenses paid. Phillips, make this happen."

It was a request/demand that Phillips knew well.

"I will do my best, sir."

As soon as he got back to his office, Phillips placed a call to Stan Grubbins and explained the deal.

"I don't know if Max will be able to get away. He is really busy."

"Did I mention the $50,000?"

"Sonny, I have a fund that is tipping close to a million dollars. $50,000 doesn't seem like all the money in the world."

JETHRO

"$100,000."

"What?" Stan asked.

"$100,000. What Mr. Collingsworth wants, Mr. Collingsworth gets. Pass that on. Sonny."

Stan got the dig and smiled. "Good for you, suit. Apparently, you still have one cojone. I'll pass the word on and let you know."

"Thank you."

"Max, Stan. I have some news."

"Good to hear from you, boss. I was just going to call you. I have some dynamite stuff I think will knock the socks off those suits you are talking to."

"How did you know…?"

"Word gets around. What's up?"

"They want to meet you."

"Who?"

"The suits."

"Boss, I don't have time to…"

"How about for $100,000?"

"Wh…what?"

"That's what they are offering your fund if you will allow them to fly you from there to here and back. One day. All expenses paid."

"Wow, $100,000. That can help fund some low-interest loans for these folks."

"You bet. And, it is only for a day."

"One condition."

"What's that?"

"Priscilla comes, too."

"Should be no problem. When can you come?"

"This is Tuesday. How about Thursday?"

"It's your ballgame, Max. You set the rules."

"There's a small private field just a little east of Eureka. I'll phone you the coordinates. Thursday, noon," he declared.

"Got it. Will confirm as soon as I call the suits."

"And, boss, make sure there is a registered check waiting for me."

"Will do, Max. Sit tight."

When Max got off the call with Stan, he found Priscilla, who was reviewing some of the footage.

"Guess what, sweetheart?"

"Max, with you, I might need a hundred guesses and still not come close to what you have in mind."

"We are going to New York."

"What?"

"Seems the suits want to meet me. How about that? And they are sweetening the deal by donating $100,000 to our relief fund."

"Max, I never would have guessed that in a million years, but Max, I have nothing to wear."

"That's the best part. I will arrange for the meeting to be around 6 pm. They are sending a private plane for us, and we should land in New York around 1. That gives you a couple of hours to shop with a credit card that has no limit. How does that sound?"

"But, Max, suppose they don't... you know... like me?" she muttered.

"Are you kidding? They will love you. Trust me on this."

"Well... if you think..."

"I do think, and it's going to be great!"

Doris Grubbins appeared for her first day of work in the mailroom. 8:30 sharp.

"Stop staring, and tell me what I am supposed to do in this rat hole."

The team had received word that the boss's daughter would be helping out in the mailroom and not to go easy on her. That was an order.

"You can start with that stack of mail. Sort it according to departments, then to the person the mail is addressed to."

"Don't you have a machine or something to do that?" she complained.

"Boss's orders."

Those words chilled her to the bone. "I... I'll get right to it. Can I use that desk?"

"Sure."

So, for the next most boring two hours of her life, Doris Grubbins sifted with $200 fingernails through the unending pile of mail. Finally, she came to the final piece and placed it in its proper place. A little smug, having accomplished her task, she was quickly found to her profound displeasure that the early afternoon mail had just come in and needed to be sorted.

Heaving a sigh of unfairness, she knew there was no alternative and fell to the task she had just completed. But, a strange thing happened along the way. Doris discovered a better and faster way to sort the mail. It came to her in a flash, and she was looking for an opportunity to test it. As fellow workers expected her to bitch and moan throughout the process, they were amazed when they saw her smile as her hands flashed from the stack to the sections she had cordoned off.

When she was done in a time no one could have anticipated, she was surprised by a round of applause.

"Doris, we have never seen anything like what you just did. It was amazing. Can you teach us?"

This was absolutely the first time she had ever done anything on her own, and she was immensely proud.

'So, this is what people talk about. Doing a good day's work,' she thought. 'Not a bad feeling, I must say.'

In the days that followed, Doris actually looked forward to getting dressed appropriately for the sometimes dirty work of the mailroom. Her co-workers embraced her efforts and praised her for what she was doing. She made several suggestions that streamlined several functions and made everything more efficient. This allowed for some banter between workers that kept the mood light, and time went by much faster.

"Say, Doris, some of the people are getting together at Diego's for some drinks and nachos. Would you like to come?"

Three weeks ago, Doris Grubbins wouldn't have been caught dead in some dive. But, this new Doris smiled broadly and said, "Sure, as long as the first round is on me."

"Deal!"

What ensued was one of the best times the sophisticated and jaded socialite ever had. There was much laughter, no criticism, no judgment. Well, one over-served patron decided to ridicule the daughter of the publisher of the Gazette.

A big fellow whose balance was questionable got into Doris' face and asked in bad breath, "So, you decided to slum with the rest of us, society girl." The tone was nasty and insulting. He was big, but Theodore, Larry, and Eddie were much bigger. They surrounded the inebriate and demanded an apology for their coworker.

Doris tried to prevent a fracas.

"It's ok, Doris. We got this. Nobody comes in here and insults one of our people."

The man turned pale as he realized these fellows who were used to tossing very heavy objects around could do the same to him.

"I...I'm sorry. I didn't mean anything by it," he protested.

"Apologize." It was a demand.

"Uh... Doris..."

"That's Miss Grubbins to you," Larry corrected.

"Uh...ok. Miss Grubbins, I'm sorry if I offended you. I'm sorry."

"Sorry enough to buy a round of drinks for my friends?" she asked smugly.

The big man looked around and gulped when he saw eight other members of the group.

"Uh....sure. No trouble. No trouble at all."

When the guy paid the tab and left, Doris planted a kiss on the cheeks of each of her rescuers.

"My heroes," she muttered as they all blushed and ducked their heads. That night of bonding lasted the rest of their lives, and Doris would always remember it with a smile.

"Parson, how are things coming along?" Max asked.

"Wonderfully, Max. It's been two weeks since the first shipment arrived, and I can already tell that the energy levels are up with a lot of men who are reporting for whatever work we need done. I've organized a team of people who are good with tools to go into homes that could use a little sprucing up."

Max then slapped his forehead. "Paint!"

"What did you say, Max?"

"Pastor, if I can get the paint and brushes and stuff, do you think your gang would be interested in giving a fresh coat of paint to some of the homes?"

"Oh, what a wonderful idea! I am sure I can get a team together. That would be such a great way to brighten up their homes."

"Great! I'll get right on it," Max promised.

"Max, you have been running around like the Energizer Bunny. Slow down a little."

Max placed a call to the Sherwin-Williams company, and after a few preliminary holds, he finally spoke to the sales manager for the Arkansas region.

"Listen, this is Maxwell Longfellow and I was wondering....."

"You are that Jethro fellow, aren't you?"

"Well, yes I am. Listen, the reason for my call....."

"Man, I got to tell you I have been hanging on to every report. It is a wonderful story."

"Thank you. Actually, that's the reason for my call. I was wondering if your company would cut me a deal on a large quantity of paint."

"For what reason?"

"I want to paint the homes of these poor people. I have the labor. All I need is the paint. And, you know, brushes, rollers, or whatever is needed. I am willing to pay a fair price."

"No deal."

Max had not been prepared for such a cold shut-down.

"But, I said I could pay....."

"No, sir. If you think we would take a penny for what you want to do, you don't know Sherwin-Williams. You tell me what you need, and I'll have it there by Saturday. No charge."

"None at all?"

"None. Nothing. Nada. Zilch."

"Wow. This is more than I could have expected. Your name?"

"Charlie McGregor."

"Well, Charlie McGregor, you are going to make an awful lot of people happy. I will be sure they know how this came about."

"That's not necessary. I'm glad to do it."

"Still, your good work should not go unrecognized."

Indeed, Max called Sherwin-Williams headquarters and was surprised that people there knew who he was, and he was put through to the Regional Director.

Max explained what McGregor had offered and wanted to make sure he would not get into any trouble.

"Trouble? I'm putting him in for a promotion. You know how valuable this will be to our brand and our team? No. He did exactly the right thing, and you have our full support, and I'll take care of Charlie."

"Thanks. You are good people."

Sure enough, come Saturday, a big Sherwin-Williams truck pulled up near the Radisson. Pastor Brown summoned a crew of men that were on the spot in a matter of minutes and unloaded the hundreds of gallons of paint in every color of the rainbow.

"We didn't think everybody would want the same color, so we included a bunch. I am told, if you need more, just say the word."

"We are in your debt, young fellow. Thank you for doing this."

"Hey, Pastor, it was my pleasure. Haven't felt this good in years."

"Do you have time to stay for supper? We would love to have you."

"Hey, why not? I'd love to," he said happily.

Thursday morning, Priscilla was nervous as a prostitute in church.

"What is it, sweetheart?" Max asked.

"I...I've never been in a plane."

"What?"

"Well, where in the world do you think a girl from here would be going?"

"I didn't mean that as a criticism, hon. Not at all. It was just a surprise, that's all."

"I know. But, I am a bit nervous."

"Well, I'll be right there next to you holding your hand the entire way, if you want."

She gave a small smile of reassurance. "That will be nice," she concluded.

One of the men who had a car drove them the four miles to the airport, which wasn't actually an airport. It was a flat piece of ground that stretched for a ¼ mile. While it was not paved, it was packed-down clay that was smooth enough for a plane to take off and land.

Max said hello to the pilot, a young, handsome, blond-haired fellow of 21 or 22.

"Are you old enough to fly this thing?" Max asked, only half-joking.

"Trust me, if the suits didn't think I was capable of flying this million-dollar bird, I couldn't get within a mile of the thing. Climb aboard."

When Priscilla ducked into the luxurious plane, she gasped.

"Max, I had no idea flying could be this luxurious."

"Priscilla, don't get spoiled. This is not how the rest of the world flies. This is about as upper-end as it gets. Enjoy it."

And they did. The plane had been supplied with sandwiches and an assortment of drinks and desserts.

Max helped her get buckled in and, as promised, sat next to her, held her hand, and before they knew it, the jet snapped their heads back and they were airborne.

Max expected Priscilla to be frightened. Instead, she cried, "Whee! That was a rush!"

"You're not...?"

"Frightened? No. Not at all! It was great. Max, this is fantastic. Thank you so much for including me."

"Hey, we are a package deal. They want me, they get us. Now and always. Pure and simple."

"Have I told you I love you lately?"

"Not that I recall," he said, scratching his chin sagely.

That called for the words as well as a kiss to go with it.

Stan Grubbins was a tough old bird, but he did not find it pleasant to have to come down so hard on his only child. In fact, the days following his edict, he sort of regretted it, thinking that she would be crushed emotionally. He had no contact with her since that day of reckoning and dreaded what he might discover when they finally met again, which was inevitable since she was his daughter and they worked in the same building.

One day, he decided to slip down to the mailroom. Now, a man as big and massive as Stan Grubbins can't really "slip" around anywhere. But, he managed to quiet a few inquisitive looks by a finger to the lips and made his way to the mailroom where he heard... laughter!

Laughter? In the mailroom? The place where laughter goes to die because of the monotony? Yes. Laughter. Unmistakable. The big man stepped inside, and the laughter ceased immediately. But the last laugh to die down was from... Doris Grubbins.

"Daddy! What a pleasant surprise," she said cheerfully and sincerely.

"OK. Who are you, and what have you done with my daughter?"

"Oh, Daddy, you are so funny," she retorted without missing a beat.

"Doris, I thought I would find you crushed under a pile of mail."

The foreman, Eddie, spoke up.

"Mr. Grubbins, Doris has been a blessing. She has come up with some simple adjustments that have made things so much more efficient. Plus, she is fun to be around."

"Doris? My Doris?" he asked with utter amazement.

"Daddy, you can at least have the good manners not to be shocked that your daughter could have friends. And good ones, I might add."

A soft chorus of, "You bet," confirmed her claim.

"Well, this is a pleasant surprise," Stan said. "If you have learned your lesson, I think we can end your little penalty period."

"No."

"Did I hear you say no?"

"Yes, you did. I like it here. I feel useful, and I have a few more ideas I want to try out."

"Well, at least I'll reinstate your credit cards," Stan offered.

"No need to. I already have more clothes than I need, and I am doing okay with what you pay me here. Although, I think my friends here could use a raise. They say they haven't had one in over two years."

"I didn't know," Stan admitted.

"You know now. Are you going to do something about it?"

Everyone in the newsroom was holding their breath, waiting for the explosion. It never happened.

Instead, Stan said, "I'll see to it."

"Promise?"

"Stan Grubbins doesn't make promises. Just check your pay envelopes this Friday."

"Sorry, Daddy. That was a little too smart-alecky even for me."

"The fact that you admitted that is a sign that you really have grown into a lovely, worthwhile person."

"Thank you, Daddy. Or should I say, 'boss'?"

"Daddy is fine. Plenty fine," he said with a big satisfied smile.

Chapter 9: City of Dreams

As Max and Priscilla luxuriated in the confines of the Lear jet, the pilot announced, "The trip will take about three hours, wheels down at LaGuardia. I hope you enjoy the trip."

That was the last they heard from him, and that was fine with them. They indulged in the drinks and desserts that were in plentiful supply. Priscilla found it hard to take her nose off the window. All she could see were clouds and occasionally glimpses of land, very far down.

"Max, this is a miracle. Here we are, flying like the wind and munching on all this great food."

"And on someone else's dime. Don't forget that," Max added.

"True. I don't know if we will ever get a chance to do this again," she said with a tinge of regret.

"Priscilla, this might be as good a time as any to say a few things."

"Oh, I hope nothing bad!" she cried.

"Oh, stupid me. It's all good, trust me. I can't say for sure, but I think that when this is all over, we are going to be rich. I mean really rich."

"Really?" she asked hopefully.

"Yes. Just think, we have enough video to make a TV movie or a couple of them. I will definitely write a book. Maybe, two. That means money. Big money."

"H...how big?"

"Millions."

"Oh dear," she uttered.

"Problem?"

"I've never had money. Even a little money, until you got me that deal with Mr. Grubbins."

"Chicken feed, Priscilla. Chicken feed. Now here is the thing. Even when I get the loot, I do not intend to go on some drunken binge. The first thing we do is get a financial advisor and have that money work for us. 'Money makes money' is true. Plus, there will be a lot of people we will want to help."

"Oh, Max, that sounds so wonderful, I dare not hope too much."

"Hope away, my love, because I think it will happen pretty much that way, and we will enjoy the ride together."

"Always together," she repeated.

Before they knew it, they felt the sleek plane bank into a turn.

"Approaching landing. Seat belts, please," the pilot announced. Buckled in, Priscilla closed her eyes and held Max's hand so tightly that he thought blood would stop flowing to his fingers if they had to make a pass. But, the young pilot set the plane down like it was a gentle feather. The reverse thrusters finally brought it to a walk as it found its resting spot away from the big planes.

"You can open your eyes now, sweetheart," Max said with a smile.

"Really?"

"Yep. Time to shop. Let's go."

They thanked the pilot, who gave them a number to call whenever they wanted to fly back.

They were surprised when they were met by a liveried gentleman in a dark blue uniform holding a sign that read "Max Longfellow." They walked over, and Max introduced himself. The tall, well-built gentleman in his early 50s spoke with a military bearing. He tipped his cap and announced, "Steve Barton, sir. At your service. If you will follow me, I will take you to wherever you wish to go."

"Uh... Steve, we need to do some shopping before our meeting later."

"No problem, sir. My car and I are at your disposal."

"Yeah, but I hate to have you waiting around. I don't know how long..."

That caused a smile on the handsome, chiseled features of this most impressive fellow.

"Mr. Longfellow, if you knew what they were paying me, you would not hesitate to take as much time as you needed. Trust me, this is a wonderful gig for me."

"Well, ok. But can we make it Max and Priscilla? The 'Mr. Longfellow' thing makes me feel old."

"OK. But we need to keep that between us. The suits frown on familiarity."

"What the hell do they know in their ivory towers?"

"Agreed, but if questioned, I will deny everything," he said with a smile.

"Agreed. So, Steve, where would a beautiful woman like my Priscilla, with a no-limits credit card, go to buy some duds for this meeting?"

JETHRO

"Can't miss with Neiman Marcus," was the suggestion.

"Then, Neiman Marcus it is!"

Steve maneuvered the Lincoln limo through and around a river of yellow taxis.

Priscilla was holding on for dear life, and Max had thoughts of gangrene again. But in a matter of 15 minutes, Steve was holding the door open for them.

"Here we go. I'm sure you will find something special for the lovely woman," Steve announced in a rich baritone.

Max thought, "Damn, if I was a foot taller and had that voice, I could rule the world."

"Thanks, Steve. How will I contact you when we are through?"

"I have a parking place that has a view of the entrance. You come out, I will be there in one minute."

"OK. Again, I'm sorry for the wait."

"Max, remember 'Ka-ching!' I am making money every minute. Please don't trouble yourself."

"OK. See you."

Priscilla was wearing the best dress she owned—a blue dress that hit her at mid-calf with a wide hem. It snuggled close to her flat tummy and small waist and was a head-turner in any universe, except this one. Several well-dressed matrons seemed to think they were invisible. Priscilla started fretting and pulling at her top, which was struggling to contain her ample curves.

Max then did something he never thought he would. He held up the black Mastercard and then slammed it down on a nearby counter.

That got the attention of a thin, gray-haired woman who had the straightest back Max had ever seen.

"May I help you?" she sniffed.

"I hope so. If not, they tell me this card works just as well at Bergdorf Goodman," Max said in his most snobbish tone.

"That won't be necessary. I am Mrs. Goodwin. I will be glad to help with your needs."

"Mrs. Goodwin, this is my wife, Priscilla. Here is the deal. You outfit her with something really special for a meeting we are going to have with the suits at CBS later. Also, fill out whatever a woman needs for different occasions."

"Very well, sir," the 60ish woman, who was as tall as Priscilla but weighed an anemic 125 pounds, said as she led Priscilla toward the back. Max stopped her with, "One more thing, Mrs. Goodwin. I don't want my wife to see the price tags. Get her whatever you think is best, regardless of the cost. That card has no limit."

She looked unimpressed and said, "Sir, that is not the first black Mastercard I have ever seen. Your wife is in good hands. Incidentally, it might not hurt for you to visit our men's department."

Max then realized he really didn't have anything suitable to wear for the meeting. Going in as a dusty character from the wilds of Arkansas might not be the best look. So, he went over to the men's department and was immediately confronted by the most handsome and stylish man he had ever seen. Tall, well-built, immaculate haircut, impeccable pinstriped suit, white shirt, and paisley tie. The guy could have stepped off the cover of GQ.

"May I help you?" he said, looking down from his lofty six-foot-two.

"Yes. I need some clothes."

"I'm sure you do," he said in a pinched tone.

'Thank God he sounds like a girl,' Max thought. 'Mr. Perfect would have been hard to take for more than 15 minutes.'

"I need a really good suit. I have an important meeting this afternoon. Can you outfit me...?"

"Terrence."

"Terrence, then. What would you suggest?"

"You look to be a 40 regular."

"I guess so, but I wouldn't swear to it," Max quipped.

No response from the dour mannequin.

"Follow me."

Max trailed behind this poster child for high culture and felt like he should be back with Jethro. But they came to an area that contained a fitting room, which had a full-length mirror.

Terrence brought several suits he thought might be appropriate. Before he handed a pair of trousers to Max, he insisted on measuring the leg length.

Max shut his eyes, fearing any familiarity. But, apparently, Max was not Terrence's type. One quick check of the tape and he simply muttered, "Thought so."

Max slipped out of his slacks and into what he knew was going to be one expensive suit. As soon as the smooth material touched his skin, he sighed, "So, this is what luxury feels like."

Except for having to take up the trousers, Max loved the suit. The jacket fit him perfectly, and even in his yellow T-shirt, he thought he looked snazzy.

"I like it, Terrence. I'll take it."

"Do you not want to know the price?"

Then Max had the greatest satisfaction of coming up with the perfect answer at the perfect time, not sometime later when he would chastise himself by saying, "Damn, why didn't I think of that then?"

Not this time. With as much nonchalance as he could muster, he said, "Terrence, if you have to look at price tags, you have no business shopping here."

That stopped the perfect specimen in his tracks and elicited a smile of approval.

"Exactly."

Now, on better footing, Terrence filled out the other parts of the ensemble, including shoes, socks, and the whole nine yards.

"You might as well throw in a few sweaters and shirts, Terrence. Also, a couple of pairs of slacks. Whatever you think I need."

Terrence could do math. He knew he was running up a tab that would be the envy of every salesman in the place.

Terrence followed Max up to check-out, where they met Priscilla, who looked a little harried but happy.

"Max! It was so wonderful. Mrs. Goodwin was amazing. I think we have some nice things."

"Ahem. We don't have 'nice' things at Neiman Marcus," corrected the stern woman, who then betrayed herself by smiling.

"It was a pleasure to serve you, madame."

"Priscilla, please."

"Yes, Priscilla. A lovely name for a lovely woman."

"Is it ok to wear this outfit? Like now?"

"It's yours and fits you perfectly. Why not?"

"As for you, Max, I suggest you slip into those slacks that fit you so well. Maybe one of those shirts and cashmere sweaters?"

"Great idea, Terrence. I look like a gnome next to my beautiful wife. And thanks for adjusting the suit on such short notice."

"No problem."

Ten minutes later, a transformed Maxwell Longfellow appeared. He was 'casual chic.' Even Terrence smiled in approval.

"Now, that is more like it."

Max said, "OK, time to break the bank. Tote it up, Mrs. Goodwin and Terrence, but please don't tell me what the tab is. Can you do that?"

"For you, sir, absolutely," said Terrence.

Max and Priscilla were forbidden from carrying their purchases to the waiting car.

"We have interns for such things. Do come again," Terrence and Mrs. Goodwin said in tandem.

As soon as they started to blink in the afternoon sun, Steve was there with the limo.

"Hey Steve. All done."

"You folks look great."

"Thanks. Listen, we still have some time before the meeting. Where is a good place to grab a bite to eat?"

"This is the Big Apple. Wave a stick and you'll find someplace. But since this is the ladies' first trip, might I suggest Tavern on the Green?"

"Oh Max! That sounds lovely."

"Then, Tavern on the Green it is. Onward, Steve!"

Max and Priscilla were like two children, giddy with the excitement of enjoying Christmas-like delight in each new view of the most interesting city in the world. And, from a private limo to boot!

Steve assured them that he would be within hailing distance, so no worries.

Priscilla gasped at the sheer beauty of the view of Central Park from the iconic tavern, which was world-famous.

"It's like a fairyland, Max," Priscilla sighed.

"I agree, sweetheart. This isn't Grand Rapids. This is like nowhere I have ever been, so don't think I am this great world traveler. I am just as agog at these incredible skyscrapers as you are. I am so glad that we are experiencing this together. Frankly, if it wasn't for you, it wouldn't mean much. But with you, everything is magnified. I am truly happy that I found you, my sweet."

"Max, I am convinced that you are a poet. The way you can string words together just mesmerizes me. And I am so grateful that Jethro brought us together."

Max was quiet for a few moments.

"What is it, Max?"

"Jethro. That is the first time I even gave him a thought. And yet, he, or they, have been the focus of our lives almost every day."

"You miss him, don't you?"

"I... I guess I do," Max admitted. "When I am around him, I seem to be in another realm. Almost like a fairy tale, not knowing what might be coming next, but always with the possibility of it being mind-blowing. Yes, I miss him, but right now, I am concentrating on making memories we will be able to recall when we go home."

It was Priscilla's turn to be quiet.

"What?"

"Home. You said 'when we go home.' Which home is that? Eureka or Grand Rapids?"

"Oh gee, Priscilla, I really have not given any thought to that. There is still so much to do. Let's just see how things shake out. OK? There will be plenty of time to make decisions. For right now, I am looking over this great menu."

So, they enjoyed a most delicious luncheon with the most beautiful view from their vantage point.

"Hate to tell you, Priscilla, but we need to get to the hotel to get ready for the meeting."

"Are you sure you want me to come?" Priscilla asked with a bit of worry.

"Absolutely! You are a big part of this and it will be good for them to have your impressions as well as mine. No. I need you there. I'm not too sure how cocky I will be with all those suits."

"You'll do fine, Max. I know it."

Meanwhile, back 'home,' Eureka was in the process of a makeover, and there was a sense of holiday about it. It seemed that every able-bodied man and boy was wearing a white painter's cap. Under the organizing eye of Pastor Brown, it was like a swarm of worker bees when people arrived at a dingy shack, some of which may have never been painted before. And now, the owner was asked, "So what color would you like your kitchen? We have a variety of colors to choose from. Army yellow? Good choice. Now, just stand back and we'll be done in a jiffy." And they were. Time and again, a team of five or six very happy people would arrive at a dingy brown home, only to leave it a few hours later, gleaming with a new coat of paint. The effect on the residents, who had spent most of their time scraping out a meager living with turnips and whatever they could coax out of the hard land, was nothing short of transformative. Their spirits raised, their stomachs full, they looked outward at how they might help their neighbors. There was a revival of Saturday square dances that had been such an integral part of this community until it fell on hard times. But now, with the increased nourishment, came new determination to improve their lives. Some agronomists visited and suggested certain steps that could make the most of the soil they had to work with. They also suggested some crops that were more conducive to the clay-like soil. Tools and machinery were now available, as well as new types of seed. The result was a thriving community humming with activity of all kinds. Most of all, they had hope. Such a simple thing, yet something most of these people didn't have. Until now. Eureka was still quite a bit off the beaten path of places people might consider visiting. There really wasn't a lot to see. No memorials. No grand statues. No historic mementos. However, there was Jethro. That alone could start a stampede if the word got out that he was in these parts. The trick now was for the town to prosper, but not with an influx of outside people. Pastor Brown and some town elders wondered how Max might be able to thread that needle. But, as one, they agreed that if anyone could figure it out, it would be their Max. They were already claiming him as their savior, for it was he who got the powers that be to cough up the money to get things going. And it was insightful and suspenseful reports that kept thousands of people so interested that they were glad to donate to the fund. Yes, if there was a statue erected, it would be of Maxwell S. Longfellow.

Steve dropped Max and Priscilla off at 45 Rockefeller Plaza, within walking distance of their meeting site. It was after both had showered and were preparing to dress in their new outfits that it hit Max.

"Priscilla! These people are used to getting reports from a down-and-dirty reporter."

"So?"

"So, am I going to look down-and-dirty in those new clothes I bought?"

"Oh, I didn't think of that, Max. What do you suggest?"

"I'll save the fancy duds for another occasion. For now, let's get into our regular clothes. They will be a lot more comfortable anyway."

"But Max, I was looking forward to dressing up for you," Priscilla pouted.

"Sweetheart, I promise you will get opportunities to show off that fabulous figure in this great outfit."

So, in their comfortable Eureka clothes, the pair presented themselves to a receptionist at the CBS Studios, who immediately ushered them into a huge boardroom. Around a rectangular table made of dark walnut that could have served as a banquet table for King Arthur and his Knights, sat about 20 executives of various grades. It was very daunting, and Priscilla slipped her hand into Max's.

"Mr. Longfellow, welcome!" was the hearty greeting from Charles Collingsworth, CEO in charge of special programming.

Max raised his right hand in a general greeting and said, "Hi. This is my wife and partner, Priscilla."

"Welcome, Priscilla. So lovely to have you both here. Please sit. Make yourselves as comfortable as you can be in this very formal environment. Please help yourselves to the refreshments."

"Thank you, but we had a late lunch. What can I do for you, ladies and gentlemen?"

"Well, we thought you might provide some first-hand information on this 'Operation Jethro' business."

"What would you like to know?"

"Well, just who is this Jethro? From your reports, he is a cross between the Loch Ness monster and Bigfoot. Is that just hype?"

"No, he is not. And I don't know if you have been informed, but I believe there are two Jethros. One is about 15 years older than the other, but you would not be able to tell who is the older. It is like they are identical, which is impossible. My wife encountered one Jethro, and I encountered the other, and their identities are exactly the same. Same height, weight, both wearing blue overalls, same placid face."

"So, how can you tell them apart?" asked one executive.

"One Jethro has a male wolf, and the other an identical female wolf that is never more than a step away."

"Wolves? Is that common in the Ozarks?" asked another.

"I have come to believe that there are animals of all sorts in the Ozarks. You need to realize we are talking about an area of some 50,000 square miles that takes in parts of four or five states. I would venture to say that there are portions of the Ozarks that are as remote as if you were on another planet."

"Fascinating!" someone murmured.

"What do you think the Jethros represent, Mr. Longfellow?" another asked.

"I've been trying to figure that out. So far, they seem like guardians of the animals. They have accepted the responsibility of making sure that the animals are well-fed and cared for. I don't know where they get the feed and foodstuffs for such a variety of animals. We are talking bears, mountain lions, deer, moose, snakes..."

"Snakes?" someone said with disgust.

"They are part of the circle of life and are respected for the role they play in the ecosystem," Max explained.

"Where do you think the Jethros get this feed and foodstuffs?"

"You know, I asked him once. He said, 'It is provided.' You must remember that conversations with Jethro have been limited, and he usually does not expand on answers to my questions. I get the feeling that he is operating at a different level than the rest of us."

"Would you enlarge on that, sir?" asked the CEO.

"I don't know. I just get this feeling that they know things we don't. They seem to be so in tune with nature that they wear it like a glove. I remember the first time I saw Jethro. The thing that impressed me most was the absolute silence in the area."

"What do you mean, silence?" asked someone.

"I mean, one minute you have birds, bugs buzzing, and animals making various sounds. Then...silence. Dead silence. Nothing moves or utters a sound. It was like the world was holding its breath. It was the most unnerving experience I ever encountered. And it happened twice."

"What do you think it means?"

"Listen, I am a journalist, and this is way above my pay grade. Anything I can offer is pure speculation."

"Yes, but no one knows this Jethro better than you. He seems to have trusted you."

"Yes, until some lunkhead among you almost queered the deal by doing a flyover. As soon as that happened, the Jethros disappeared. Well, they are there, somewhere. But if they don't want to be found, no one will ever find them. When I go back, I will have to try to reestablish that trust. We are doing that by the fund you folks are helping to spearhead. Jethro cares as much about his people as he does the animals, and his instruction to give those good people a leg up made him happy. Well, as happy as a being like Jethro can be."

"You speak as if he could be some sort of deity."

"To those in the area, that's what he is. They claim him as a protector. Faith is a funny thing. People don't need concrete proof if they believe someone has their best interests at heart. And that's the way they feel about Jethro. Look, I have barely scratched the surface of the legend of Jethro. For all I know, these two that I am dealing with are only the last two of a long line of Jethros. I've heard tales from some very old codgers who heard of Jethro when they were children. And that could have been 80 years ago."

A murmur of amazement rippled through the room.

"So, this mystery is not going to be over anytime soon?"

"I can't say. I get the feeling that something weird or special is about to happen."

"Why do you say that?"

"Well, according to many sources, this is the first time the two Jethros have been this close together. I don't know if there will be a merging or something. Again, this is mystery stuff. I wish I could provide more facts, but with Jethro, you get only what he will give you. That's why I am anxious to get back."

"We can understand that, Maxwell, so let us make clear what our thinking is."

"Please do."

"We intend to continue to ride this wave of interest in Jethro. It has done wonders for some of our affiliate shows and has been the subject of much discussion when this is over."

"Like what?"

"We would like to sign you to a contract that stipulates that any information and material will be funneled through corporate for possible promotional products like movies, made-for-TV movies, and any number of articles and books."

"No."

"Pardon?"

"If you think I am going to sell out the Jethros, you are greatly mistaken."

"But we are talking millions of aid to that region."

"We are doing pretty well with the donations from a lot of regular folks who are proud to be part of Project Jethro. You may remember my boss, Stan Grubbins. He has connections that have been very supportive of our cause. He is willing to wait and see how this all plays out. Jethro will be calling the shots as far as the timeline is concerned. No one else."

"Mr. Maxwell, you are making a big mistake. An opportunity like this comes along maybe once in a lifetime to a journalist like you."

"Oh, I agree. And had you made this proposal when I first sighted Jethro, I might have considered it. But Jethro has changed me. My thinking is broader and takes in a lot more than just the story. About that. Not to be arrogant, is there anyone among you who doubts that I will get at least a six-figure book deal out of this? Maybe even be up for a Pulitzer? I have my beautiful wife, more friends than I ever thought I would have, and the most interesting job in the world. So you'll pardon me if I pass."

"And you would risk losing our support?"

"And would you really risk the PR fallout from that decision? 'Corporate pulls the plug on relief aid because total control was denied.' I'm not an adman, but even I could write something like that. Easy."

The CEO hastily cut in and said, "I think we might have gotten on the wrong track. Of course, we will continue our support. As a matter of fact, I say we boost it by ten percent."

"15% would be better," Max quipped.

That caused a big smile on the face of the distinguished executive.

"Mr. Longfellow, you have the heart of a pirate, and I admire that. 15% it is. I want to thank you for making the trip here."

"You may think twice about that after you see the tab we ran up on that black Mastercard you provided."

"Oh?"

"I thought we needed to dress up for this meeting, and before we came, we stopped off at Nieman Marcus and got a few things for my wife and me. Then I realized it would be more effective if you saw us in our work clothes."

"That seems a shame. I mean that your beautiful wife won't have a chance to display some of her purchases."

"Yeah, but thanks for the duds. I'm sure it's not going to pinch your bottom line."

Then, one of the minor executives whispered something in the CEO's ear that caused an immediate smile.

"Mr. Maxwell, do you have to get back right away?"

"Well, we were planning on leaving right after this meeting."

"My assistant tells me that there is a charity gathering about two hours from now. It is a gala affair, and we would like to invite you and your wife to attend. It'll give you a chance to show off your new 'duds,' as you call them."

Priscilla's eyes started to sparkle, and she squeezed Max's hand.

He looked at the desire in her eyes.

"What the hell. It's your jet. Sure, we will be glad to attend."

"Great! Wonderful! Let us adjourn now, and we will see you a little later. We will alert your driver with the details."

"His name is Steve. And you guys have yourself a winner in that guy. Just saying."

"Duly noted," said the CEO.

Chapter 10: New Beginnings

Max took Priscilla by the hand and said, "C'mon, sweetheart. We need to have Mrs. Goodwin pick you out a gown that will knock their socks off."

"But Max, we have already spent so much…"

"They have. And they have plenty left. Trust me."

"Steve, we need to get back to Nieman Marcus. Pronto."

"Really?"

"Yes, there is this big gala, whatever that is, tonight, and the suits want to show us off. So, we need to get something suitable for my beautiful wife."

"Well, I'm sure whatever she wears will put all those other women to shame," the big man said.

"My sentiments, exactly," said Max.

"Incidentally, you didn't say anything to the suits. You know, about me?"

"Why do you ask?"

"I just got a call from my supervisor that I was promoted to the upper echelon of chauffeurs."

"What does that mean?"

"It means that I will be among the few drivers who will chauffeur dignitaries and visiting heads of state. That is the most coveted assignment in the business. Are you sure you didn't say anything?"

"Me? I'm a little journalist from the boonies. Who will listen to me?" Max said.

But Steve thought differently and gave some silent thanks to Max.

"Mrs. Goodwin, I bet you didn't expect to see us so soon."

"Why, Mr. Longfellow, what can I do for you?"

"I need a knock-out gown for my lovely Priscilla. We have this fancy ball or something tonight, and I want to give those suits something to remember us by. Got any gowns that might fill the bill?"

The refined, dignified, ramrod-straight woman sniffed, "This is Nieman Marcus, sir. Of course, we have what is necessary. Priscilla, is it? Please follow me."

Max started to follow until the school marm instructed, "You. Stay here until called."

Max stopped dead in his tracks and obeyed meekly, looking for a chair to park himself until summoned.

Priscilla followed like a little girl. They arrived in the rear of the store where there were just a few gowns. But Mrs. Goodwin already had a good idea of what would fill the bill. She brought Priscilla two gowns, one of which she knew would not work but needed it to set the stage for the pièce de résistance.

Priscilla slipped out of her clothes in the fitting room and wiggled into the first gown, which was a wine-colored number that was very dramatic. Perhaps a bit too much. But Priscilla took a look in the full-length mirror and couldn't believe it was her being reflected.

"This is stunning, Mrs. Goodwin."

"Yes. But not for you. Try this one."

She handed Priscilla a shimmering light green silk gown that seemed to weigh four ounces.

"Uh...Mrs. Goodwin, in case you haven't noticed, I am a pretty big girl."

"I have been doing this for more years than you have been on this earth. Trust me. Try it on."

Priscilla retired to the dressing room and wiggled into this diaphanous creation that, after she got it past her ample hips, floated into place like it was painted on her. It was skin-tight but not at all uncomfortable. As a matter of fact, it felt like she wasn't wearing anything. The gown clung to Priscilla's every curve, with the bodice being firm against her flat stomach. She was alarmed, however, at how much cleavage the square-cut neckline revealed.

"No. No. You don't go pulling up the gown. There really is not enough to cover those beauties. My dear, in the parlance of the trade, 'If you have them, flaunt them.'"

"But I feel so...exposed," Priscilla protested.

"Have you taken a good look in the mirror?"

"Well...no."

"I suggest you do so."

Priscilla, who had great bearing, stood tall and gazed at this creature wearing this gown that seemed to float on air. It fit her like a glove.

"This is most unusual, but there is not one bit of alteration required. It is...perfect," the experienced stylist confessed.

"It is rather elegant, isn't it," Priscilla said, warming to the idea.

"No. You are elegant. The dress just complements you."

"Will you be so good as to notify Max? I would hate to embarrass him in something like this."

"Madame! Nieman Marcus does not deal in 'embarrassing' clothing," Mrs. Goodwin said in all her haughty snobbishness.

"Oh, I am so sorry. I didn't mean that. I am so confused. Yesterday, I was in jeans in the Ozarks, and now here I am in one of the most exclusive dress shops in the world. It's...a...lot to take in," she sniffled.

"There, there, child. Don't fret. You are just endowed with an overabundance of beauty. Trust me. Enjoy it while you can. Someone will fetch your husband."

Thirty seconds later, Max followed a saleswoman to where Priscilla was standing in all her glory. To say he was stopped dead in his tracks would be an understatement. His eyes bulged as he swept all of Priscilla's shimmering beauty into his field of vision and his mind.

"Priscilla? Is that you?"

"Mr. Maxwell. Really!"

"I...I never saw anything more beautiful in my life. Nothing."

"Max, do you think it is too...revealing?"

"No. It is...perfect. Just...perfect," he muttered, still trying to drink in all of what he was looking at.

"Mrs. Goodwin says she thinks it would be appropriate for the gala we are to attend. And I trust her."

That made the matronly woman with the stern exterior flinch a little. 'I do believe this girl is the sweetest customer I have ever met,' she thought.

"If it's good enough for Mrs. Goodwin, it's good enough for me. Wrap it up."

"Not quite yet. A gown is only as effective as its shoes and purse. Follow me. Uh...Priscilla, be careful getting out of that gown, then meet me in the shoe department."

"Yes, ma'am," Priscilla agreed.

By the time Max and Priscilla rendezvoused with Mrs. Goodwin in the shoe department, she had one of her clerks provide several suitable shoes to complement the gown. Since Priscilla was already 5'8", she didn't want anything that made her look more like a giantess.

"A medium heel, perhaps?"

Max said, "Hey, don't worry about towering over me. Get what is best for the outfit."

"Good man," Goodwin muttered.

So, they settled on a high heel that was just short of a spike.

"I can't get over it," Priscilla wondered. "I would expect these to be so uncomfortable, but they are quite comfy."

"They should be. They cost $500," Goodwin commented dryly.

"Oh my gosh! No. I could never..."

"Hey, babe, it's a once-in-a-lifetime deal. Go for it," Max stated.

"Are you sure?"

"It's their money. Why not?"

"And here is the perfect beaded purse to go with it, and you are all set," Mrs. Goodwin concluded.

"Oh, now if I only had time to do something with this mess of hair," Priscilla complained.

"Don't touch it!"

The remark rang out like a shot and caught Max and Priscilla off guard.

"I am sorry for the outburst, but you have a rich head of hair most women would kill for."

"But it is long and not at all styled," Priscilla protested.

"Yes, and it flows in golden waves to your shoulders. Priscilla, you look like a goddess. Don't diminish your appearance with some cheap hairdo. You are gorgeous. That should be enough for anyone."

Max said, "I totally agree. So, let's wrap this baby up and get going."

"Mrs. Goodwin, I can't thank you enough," Priscilla said sincerely. Then she took the dignified woman by surprise by engulfing her in a big hug. They left a bewildered but smiling woman in their dust as they headed for the hotel to change.

Stan Grubbins was a happy man. His ace reporter was in New York making nice with the suits. Circulation and revenue were up as the interest in the Jethros still burned hot. And he had a date. The first one in a very long time. "Too long," he thought.

'What the hell is the protocol nowadays?' He decided to play all odds, so he picked up a big box of candy and had the florist make up a huge bouquet.

"Flowers and candy. Unbeatable combination. At least, I hope so. Plus, a reservation at a swanky French restaurant. That ought to do it," he hoped.

He rang the bell at the apartment, and the door was quickly opened by a very pretty girl who was in anything but dressy clothes.

"Daddy! How great to see you. Come in."

Stan walked in confused.

"Weren't we scheduled to go to dinner?"

"Yes, we were and how sweet of you to bring me candy and flowers. But I thought it would be more fun if we just stayed in and I'd fix dinner for us."

"You? Cook? Since when?"

"Since I realized how expensive food and eating out can be. A girl has to watch her expenses, you know," she said as she checked something in the oven. Clad in jeans and a sweatshirt, her auburn hair in a careless ponytail and barefoot, Stan thought that she looked like a teenager. And he smiled.

"When you say dinner, what are we talking about?"

"I have had two prime rib eyes marinating all day. The grill on the patio is ready, and I made a ton of buttered mashed potatoes. And, if you don't mind, you could fix a mixed green salad. I know you really don't like vegetables with your steak. 'They just get in the way of the spuds,' I remember you saying."

"I didn't think you were listening," he said gently.

"I listened. Sometimes, I pretended not to because I wanted to prove I was independent and didn't need any advice."

"Well, I'm going to postpone the reservation at Chez Pierre. This is so much better. But I want a rain check on taking you out to dinner."

"Deal. Now, kick off your shoes, loosen your tie, and make yourself useful in the kitchen. Oh, and there is plenty of beer in the fridge."

"Now, you have done it!" he said happily.

So, for the next 15 minutes, Stan worked side by side with his daughter as he combined several kinds of lettuce, some radicchio, and some croutons, as he chatted with Doris, who was whipping a cauldron of potatoes.

"Daddy, I know the chefs say that a steak needs to 'rest' for a few minutes after taking it off the grill. I don't buy that. I want you to slap those steaks on that grill and in eight minutes I want mine plopped on my plate. Word of warning. There will be no conversation for five minutes after that first bite. House rules. You good with them?" she snapped.

"Absolutely, captain. I am off to do my steak duties. Will report back forthwith," he said, and they both broke out in laughter.

What followed was the best dinner Stan had enjoyed in he didn't know how long. The conversation was casual and informative, dotted with frequent bouts of laughter.

"Doris, I must tell you this is so much better than dinner at Chez Pierre would ever be. I don't think they would approve patrons eating in their stocking feet."

"I have enjoyed it, too, Daddy. I forgot how funny you are with all your newspaper stories. And the way you are managing the Jethro thing is remarkable."

"You know, Max is a much better reporter than I ever gave him credit for."

"I could have told you that, but I was just a silly girl wrapped up in her own delusions of what she wanted out of a man and life."

"So, you are... okay with Max? You know, the marriage and all?"

"Yes, I am. I am happy for him. He worked hard for years at what looked like a dead-end job. He deserves his success."

"Wow, Doris, I don't mind telling you how relieved I am upon hearing that. I love you and didn't want to see you hurt, and that's where that was heading."

"Yeah, I realize that. I have grown in the past few months. I have less now and am happier than I have been in a long time."

"Sweetheart, you know you can have those credit cards anytime you want."

"No, thank you. That raise you gave to all of us in the mailroom is taking care of expenses. I like the independence, to tell you the truth."

"I understand, and I am proud of you, but if you ever need anything, I mean anything, you know I am always here. Understand?"

"I know, Daddy. You are one of my constants. Kind of like the sun. So, you'd better take good care of yourself. I want you around for a long time."

"Doris, you have given me every reason to want to stick around. Now, if you could just find someone..."

An enigmatic smile.

"Am I missing something?" he asked curiously.

"Well, remember Eddie in the mailroom? One of the guys that came to my defense?"

"Eddie. Eddie. Yes, I remember. Big guy, blond, handsome. That Eddie?"

"That Eddie," she smiled.

"How long has this been going on?"

"Oh, not very long. We just seem to hit it off. Casual and easy. He is not uptight, and we are in no rush. We're having fun."

"That's what young people are supposed to do. Have fun."

"What about you, Dad?"

"What about me?"

"Isn't there anyone that you might like to spend some time with?"

"Hey, I'm almost 70. My time has come and gone, and I'm good with that."

"I'm not," the daughter stated defiantly.

"You're not?"

"No. Damn, Daddy, you are more vital and more fun than half the men I know that are young enough to be your grandsons. You got to get out there. You have so much to offer."

"Have you taken a good look at your old man recently? I am about 40 pounds overweight, and playing tennis like I used to would definitely cause a heart attack."

"So, let's get you in shape."

"Wh...what?"

"C'mon, Daddy. It will be fun. I have a joint membership at this club I go to. Come and try it out. Please."

The combination of the earnest look on the face of his newly hatched daughter, plus the glimmer of hope that there still might be some life left in this old dog, made him say, "Damn it! I'll do it! But, if you want to separate yourself from this old codger, I'll understand."

"Not a chance. You are my father, and I will always be proud of you. Oh, this is going to be such fun!"

And it was. More than Stan could have imagined.

Doris bought him some workout clothes and had Ivan, a personal trainer, design some exercises for Stan.

"Doris, I appreciate your setting up my lessons with Ivan, but did you have to get the biggest, handsomest Swede to train me? I look like some washed-up pretzel next to him."

"Just give yourself some time. You'll see how things will shape up."

She was right, of course. Through diligent training three days a week and a modified diet, Stan started to see the pounds melt away. Plus, he got hooked on the exercises. A normally strong guy to start with, he made tremendous progress in three short months. Doris was so proud of him, and he had a new outlook on life. His energy levels were higher, and everything seemed new to him.

"So, this is what being healthy feels like," he thought. "I like it."

Apparently, so did several senior women who attended Pilates classes in another part of the gym.

One day, as Stan was heading for the showers, a white towel hanging around his neck, dabbing at some sweat, he heard a very feminine voice say, "Lookin' good."

He was startled and looked around to see whom the compliment was intended for.

Then his eyes lighted on a woman with short gray hair and twinkling blue eyes.

Stan pointed to himself and asked, "Me?"

"Yes, big fella. I've been watching your progress. I haven't seen that much determination in a long time. It is very impressive. Incidentally, my name is Marissa. Marissa Danforth."

"Well, Marissa Danforth, it is a pleasure to meet you. Stan Grubbins."

The sixty-something woman was about 5'7" and seemed like she could have been an athlete in her day. Stan got that impression by watching how gracefully she moved.

"You wouldn't be some kind of athlete, would you?"

"Oh, I haven't been called that for a long time," she demurred.

"But it's true, right?"

"Well, I have been known to hit a golf ball pretty well."

"Knew it! You have the moves of an athlete. I used to play a little football back in my college days."

"Linebacker, right?"

"H...how could you know that?"

"A guy built like you is born to rush the quarterback."

"You know football?"

"Cowboys through and through," she said with no apologies.

"What the heck is with those guys? On paper and even on the field, they seem like they have all the weapons in the world. Then come the playoffs, and they don't show up."

She heaved a sigh. "It is the curse we have to live with, but they are responsible for some of the most incredible plays ever. I love them. What about you?"

"It used to be the Packers, but I haven't really followed them much."

"Too bad. Sunday afternoon wouldn't be the same without football," she said.

"You watch Sunday football?"

"Yes. Is that strange?"

"Do you sometimes have a... beer to go along with that?"

"Of course! What is football without a brewski?"

"Oh, I didn't think they made women like you," Stan said wondrously.

"You've been out of the dating loop, haven't you?"

"Is it that obvious?"

"That's not it. I just think it's a shame. You look and sound like a guy who likes to have a good time doing simple things."

"Wow. Have you been talking to my daughter?"

"Oh, did I strike a nerve?"

"More like a chord. Football, beer, snacks, Sunday. That's like a recipe for a perfect afternoon."

"Well, the 'Boys' are playing at 4 this Sunday. I have a 101-inch screen that puts you right there in the huddle."

"Are you inviting me over? This Sunday?"

"Yes. Is that so outlandish?"

"N... No. No. Uh... Marissa, I'll admit, I don't know how this stuff works anymore."

"Tell me about it, Stan. Most people think since we are 'seniors,' life is over. I say, screw that. There is still a lot of living to do."

"I've come to understand that. I feel better now than I have in a long time. And better having met you. Think we could get a drink at the juice bar after I wash off a ton of sweat?"

"Sure, I'll save you a seat."

Stan then proceeded to take the fastest shower of his life.

Sure enough, Marissa was waiting for him at a little round, white table.

Stan's mass of white hair was still a little wet as he sat down.

"I took the liberty of ordering this orange-pineapple drink for us. I hope you don't mind."

"Not at all. That was very thoughtful of you. Thanks."

"So, Marissa, is there a Mr. Danforth?"

"Used to be," she said casually.

"Oh?"

"Mr. Danforth had a midlife crisis, and I was the victim after 32 years of marriage. Seems his secretary was able to provide what he thought he needed. He paid a mighty high price for his dalliance. I live in a very nice neighborhood with a paid-up mortgage in a very nice house."

"And him?"

"He is living alone in a two-bedroom apartment on the east side."

"And the secretary?"

"Seems he was spending so much on Viagra that he couldn't give her all the things she was accustomed to."

"Poetic justice is a bitch, if you'll pardon my French."

She chuckled and said, "I don't usually endorse profanity, but sometimes it's necessary. Now, what is your story, Stan?"

"I am the publisher of the Grand Rapids Gazette."

"Well, color me impressed. I have been on pins and needles waiting for the next installment of the Jethro saga. It's fascinating."

"It sure is. I can't wait for Max's next installment. He is quite a guy."

"I'd like to meet him sometime."

"Well, no one knows when this caper will be over. I told him to play it to the hilt, so who knows?"

"Standing request?"

"Noted. Marissa, you say you used to play some golf. I decided to permit myself some recreation time. Could you recommend a good golf teacher?"

"Sure. Me."

"You?"

"Why are you surprised? Taking lessons from a woman. Does that wrinkle your manhood?"

"No! No, not at all. I just didn't want to get you mixed up with an old guy like me that doesn't have the hand-eye coordination he used to have."

"Nobody does. But, once an athlete, always an athlete. When do you want to start?"

"Wow, you move fast. I guess I would need to get some clubs and stuff."

"I can help you with that. I have some friends at Dick's Sports Shop, and they can fit you out with suitable clubs."

Stan was thoughtful for a few moments until she asked, "What?"

"I was just wondering why you are doing all this? The football, the golf, all of it. Surely, a woman as lovely as you would set her cap for someone a lot younger and better looking than me."

He was surprised when she said, "That's true. As a matter of fact, I did try some of the younger rodeos and found them vacuous and boring. You, on the other hand, show promise of fun and growth. Someone who is enjoying this new part of their life. I could be wrong. I have been before, but a girl needs to try."

"Well, that is as honest as I could hope to hear. Frankly, I'm not sure what the rules are today, so I might screw up here and there."

She laughed a delightful laugh, showing straight white teeth, which spoke of some good dental health.

"Hey Stan, we all screw up. That's what makes us human and what makes life interesting."

"Well then, knowing the ground rules, I would love to get to know you, Marissa Danforth."

"And you, Stan Grubbins. Here's to happy times," she said as she raised her fruit drink.

Chapter 11: The Guardians' Ultimatum

Things back home were getting strange. No one knew exactly what was happening, but there seemed to be a strange vibe in the air. Like something important was about to happen. It was a feeling no one could identify, but all seemed to have an uneasy feeling. This seemed strange because the community had never been in better shape. There was enough food for everyone. Jobs, while they didn't pay much, were plentiful as people, now strong enough to farm, did exactly that, and that required many hands. The morale of the community was at its highest level, too, as people took pride in their newly painted and renovated homes. Yet, this feeling of unease persisted. Jethro had not been spotted for some time now, and people wondered if he was uneasy for some reason. They wished Max was back. They were sure he could figure something out.

Max was a couple of thousand miles away, preparing for his first gala, and probably his last. When he put on the dark blue suit and looked in the mirror, he said a silent thank you to Terrence.

"For a squirt like me, I look pretty damn good," he said to himself. "Besides, who the hell will be looking at me when I walk in with my beautiful Priscilla?"

He was right. He could have worn burlap, and no one would have noticed. When Priscilla walked into the room in her shimmering silk gown, Max had to catch his breath.

"You are the loveliest thing I have ever seen, Priscilla. Are you sure you want to be seen with a runt like me?"

"Max, you are not a runt. You are a loving man who took an Ozarks girl and gave her a taste of a life she could not even dream about. I am so proud to be your wife."

"Then, let's go knock their socks off!"

And, that's just what they did. Or she, more accurately. Now, these were sophisticated ladies and gentlemen with vast fortunes. The ladies did their best to pour on the diamonds and jewelry to dress up their appearance, but when Priscilla and Max made an appearance at the entrance of the ballroom, heads turned, conversations stopped, and more than a few overeducated mouths fell open. Priscilla might just as well have been a queen in all her regal bearing, walking sedately on the arm of her grinning escort.

Max walked toward a clutch of men he had spoken with earlier.

"Good evening gentlemen. This seems like a nice gathering."

No one heard him or saw him. They were eyeing the blond goddess he had on his arm.

"My God, Priscilla, but you are a vision," said the CEO.

Priscilla nodded demurely and said a soft "Thank you."

The women gathered around as well, and one gasped, "I don't think she is wearing a bra!"

Another quipped, "If you had tits like that, high and firm, would you wear a bra?"

"Gladys, how crude!"

"Yet, how true," she retorted.

The suits were falling all over themselves to have Priscilla sit with them. She felt like a queen but did not know how to act like one. She whispered to Max, "I don't know how I am supposed to act."

"Sweetheart, when you are as beautiful as you are, you don't have to say anything. Just enjoy the moment so you can recall it when we are back in Eureka."

"You are so smart, Max," she said proudly.

"Yeah, but I wish I was a foot taller."

"No, sweetheart. I love you just the way you are."

"Thanks, I needed that."

All heads were turned toward the table that held Priscilla, and glory fell on the suits lucky enough to have her in their midst, and they were falling all over themselves to ingratiate themselves with her. Like the queen she was, or pretended to be, Priscilla decided to play some games. She would start to say, "I wish..." and there would be five guys hanging onto the possibility it would be he who was able to please her. There was not one chance in a million that any one of them stood a Chinaman's chance of getting more than a 'thank you.'

Max was not jealous. He knew that Priscilla was having the time of her life, maybe for the only time in her life. So, he contented himself with occasional pats on her thigh under the cover of the elaborate tablecloth, and imbibed on the most expensive champagne in the world. "And, it's not costing me a dime. Life is good!"

Dinner consisted of your choice of filet mignon or chicken or salmon. Max went for the steak, but Priscilla thought it would be more dainty to pick at the salmon than grind away on a steak. It was hard for her because, being a big girl, she had a big appetite.

She whispered to Max, "Is there a chance we can get a doggy bag to go?"

"Sweetheart, if you requested it, you could get the chef to come to our rooms and cook just for you."

"Max!"

"It's true, dear. You have these guys tied up in knots. Maybe this might be the time to hit them up for an increase in their donations to our relief fund."

"But you already got them to up the percentage yesterday."

"Yeah, but there are a bunch of other guys here with pockets just as deep. It's worth a shot."

Priscilla thought about it for a bit then decided to give it a try. All they could do was say no. So, she started a conversation that caught the attention of everyone in her vicinity.

"I am so grateful to all of you who are helping us with our fund for the poor folks of the Ozarks. I know you, Mr. Collingsworth, have been very generous."

"It's nothing," he deferred modestly.

"How much?" asked Jud Peters of Conglomerates Ltd.

"I believe it was $25,000," Priscilla whispered.

"I think we can do a little better than that," he said.

Priscilla was smart enough to keep silent, but the question hung in the air.

"Let's just round it off to $100,000. How does that sound, Priscilla?"

She then took a deep breath and reached out and placed her hand on his. You would have thought that the fairy godmother had come down and kissed him on the head.

"Thank you ever so much, Mr. Peters."

This multi-billionaire who could buy and sell any ten people in the room looked like a schoolboy who had just been kissed on the cheek by his grade school girlfriend.

Max thought it was almost too comical for words, but he followed up on the offers with a printed card as to where and how the funds were to be deposited.

A bidding war of sorts got underway, and Max was afraid he would run out of cards. Later that night, in their room, the haul was close to a million dollars.

However, there was some dancing to do. Max was amazed that Priscilla was such a good dancer.

"The missionaries thought a young girl should know how to dance. I love it!"

The line of would-be partners stretched for twenty men, all eager for the opportunity to actually touch this goddess, and Priscilla accommodated all of them. Her stamina was truly impressive and did not go unnoticed by the matronly escorts of the suits, who knew there was going to be hell to pay when they got home. But, to a man, they didn't give a damn. This was as close as they were going to get to a fantasy of being in the arms of the most beautiful woman in the room. Through it all, Priscilla smiled her grand smile and genuinely enjoyed the company of the different men, most of whom squeezed a business card into her hand.

"Priscilla, if you ever need anything, I mean anything, please call me. Will you do that?"

"Oh, I couldn't...." she demurred.

"No! You must! I can help in so many ways."

"But I would hate to impose...."

"It's no imposition! I would consider it an honor."

"OK. As long as it won't cause you any trouble..."

"No trouble at all. None."

Pretty much that same story was repeated several times. By the time Priscilla left the ballroom, she had enough clout to overthrow a government if she wanted to. All she could do was shake her head and say, "Men!"

Max was also the recipient of men who had some tantalizing business opportunities.

"You know, when this is all over, look me up. We can do some business."

Max thanked everyone humbly but made no promises.

Max decided to leave on a high note. He said to the assembled execs, "We have an early flight back tomorrow, so we need to wrap this up."

There were cries of "Stay!" "One more drink!" and words to that effect.

But, in the end, every man sprang to his feet as Priscilla stood up, took Max's arm, and walked regally out of the ballroom.

Someone was heard to mutter, "Lucky son-of-a-bitch."

Once back in their room, Priscilla collapsed on the bed and said happily, "That was fantastic, Max! I will never forget it."

"Neither will they, I'm sure. You were spectacular, sweetheart. I am so glad you got a chance to show those folks what a real beauty looks like."

"Aww, you don't have to say that."

"No, but it needs to be said from time to time. And, I have a fistful of business cards that we may very well cash in on when this is all over."

"I do, too." Priscilla opened her little jeweled bag and out came some 15 or 20 cards.

"Whoa there, party girl! You may have hit the jackpot."

"Oh, stop calling me that. We had better try to get some sleep. We leave early tomorrow."

"Actually, we leave when we want to. It's our plane. Our pilot. So, sleep in if you want to."

Priscilla started undressing and folding her precious gown very carefully.

She then said, "You know, Max, this was all fantastic, but I am anxious to get back to Eureka and the folks and…Jethro. There is still some unfinished business there."

"Yeah, I hear you. I feel the same way. You can take just so much of this luxury before needing a dose of reality. I hope everything is okay back home."

Everything was not okay back home. Oh, people's needs were being met. No one was going hungry. The houses looked so much better with that fresh coat of paint. Two doctors were making the rounds to see if the children needed vaccines or other attention. Even a dentist was on hand to help people make the most of the few teeth they still had in their mouths. But, there was an air of unease that people felt but could not identify. Animals seemed to be skittish, and people's nerves seemed to be on edge. And, no one could figure out why. Meanwhile, the two Jethros started advancing toward each other. No one knew it, but it was to play a part in what was about to happen.

Stan Gubbins had to pinch himself. Not only was he and his daughter on the best terms ever, but his friendship with Marissa Danforth was blossoming into something genuinely lovely. Over the past two weeks, he and she shared football games, she got him fitted out with all of the golf club paraphernalia, and even gave him several lessons. Being such a big guy, she knew he wanted to hit the ball a mile. But, he quickly learned it's not brawn but hand speed that propels the ball, assuming you hit it squarely. He was an apt student, and after he saw his first ball get airborne, he was hooked. He went to the driving range in between lessons, and being the athlete he used to be, he tapped into the moves he used when he was in his prime.

In subsequent golf outings with just the two of them, Marissa was impressed by his rate of progress.

"Keep this up, and you'll be giving me lessons," she kidded.

"I want to thank you, Marissa. I believe I could play this game 'til I die. There is always something to learn."

"Now, you are talking like a real golf nut, just like me."

After a round of golf, it was delightful to relax in the lounge, have a drink, talk about the round, and just chat.

Then, came the day that Stan asked Marissa if she would go to dinner with him.

"We've shared dinners, Stan."

"Yes, but I would like to take you to a proper restaurant with tablecloths and waiters and all we have to do is have people serve us. Please."

"OK. Far be it for me to pass up a free meal," she quipped.

She saw that the remark stung and then she knew that Stan Grubbins might be serious about her. She did some soul-searching and discovered that she cared for him, too. She looked forward to his always cheerful attitude and his happy-go-lucky way about things. Yes, she would really like to go to dinner with Stan Grubbins.

Steve was on hand to carry Max and Priscilla to the private portion of LaGuardia Airport just before 10 a.m. As he handed them over to the pilot, he thanked Max again for putting in a good word for him with the suits.

"I want you to know I really appreciate your good word, Max, and should you come back to New York, give me a call. I will arrange to take you wherever you need to go."

"Thanks, Steve. It's been a pleasure having you as our driver. Good luck."

Soon, they were buckled in and airborne. The pilot had restocked the plane with all manner of goodies.

Priscilla said, "Max, I had a most wonderful time, but I am anxious to pick up Jethro's trail."

"I hear you, sweetheart. Our objective was to find Jethro and see what his connection was to the Ozarks. I got to believe they are happy with how their people have improved their lives, so we have that going for us."

"Yes, but with Jethro, we are dealing with, well, kind of an unknown. I mean, we really don't know what their power is or where it comes from or even what is their purpose. So many questions."

Pastor Brown and a contingent of others were on hand to greet the conquering couple.

"It is good to have you back in the fold," the pastor said as Priscilla gave him a hug.

"And, you couldn't have come back at a more propitious time."

"What do you mean, Pastor?"

"Max, there is an unsettling vibe in the air and we have not been able to figure it out. It's as if a storm is coming. The animals are nervous and jump at the least noise. People are on edge, too. People have had arguments of the most silly type. Something is not right, Max."

"Yeah, I'm sensing that, too. I think it's time for us to hunt for Jethro."

Priscilla and Max got into their 'hunting clothes' and set off for where they last saw Jethro. They had no plan except to scour as much area as they could before the sun went down. As usual, to cover more territory, they split up and went in opposite directions. Each had the warning whistle around their necks. It was Priscilla who spotted a Jethro first. As usual, he wasn't there one moment and in full view the next. Priscilla noticed this was the Jethro with the male wolf, her Jethro.

"Jethro! Hello. I missed seeing you. We were in New York raising money for the relief fund."

Jethro did not respond but did not seem displeased. It was as if he was listening to something. Priscilla noticed that birds stopped singing and any animals that might have been in the area were also silent.

Priscilla was about to ask a question when he said, "It is time." And then, he was gone. Just vanished, wolf and all. Priscilla thought she might have been hypnotized or something. She headed in the direction she thought Jethro went, which was toward Max. He had just had his encounter with a Jethro and was not able to learn anything about the vibe that was almost palpable now.

Priscilla arrived and had a brief conference with Max that availed nothing.

"Sweetheart, we are observers now. Make sure the camera is primed and ready to go and take every shot as long as Jethro is on the scene."

"Got it, Max," she said.

And, almost on cue, they watched something they never thought they would see: both Jethros approaching each other slowly and steadily. Their eyes were fixed on each other and the two wolves were at the respective sides of their masters.

Max breathed, "They are exactly alike. No difference, although one must be 15 years older than the other."

Slowly, so slowly, they closed the distance between them until they were standing a foot apart. Max and Priscilla held their breath, as did the animals in the vicinity. The Jethros had eyes only for each other. Finally, they each stepped forward and then it happened. There was a blinding flash of light that emitted all the colors of the rainbow. There was a sizzling sound as if electricity was passing between them. The entire area was lit as if by 100 Roman Candles. Then, just as quickly, the light show was over.

Priscilla and Max had reflexively squinted at the bright light, but now they opened their eyes wide and saw...nothing. Both Jethros were gone, along with their wolves. How so much flesh could disappear in the blink of an eye baffled Max.

Just as they were getting ready to leave, another surprise: both Jethros showed up suddenly.

"You have questions," one of them said. It was a statement.

"Yes, we do. What just happened?"

"At an appointed time, it is necessary for us to combine forces to maintain power."

"What do you need that 'power' for?"

"Some animals need help only we can provide. We are Guardians of these mountains."

"How long have you been doing this?"

"Time means little to us. We do what we are charged to do."

"Are there others like you?"

"Yes."

"How many?"

"As many as necessary."

"Do you have a message for the people who see this?"

"Yes. Take care of my land and its animals."

"And, suppose people don't?" Max asked.

A darkness fell on the countenance of the placid face.

"It would not be wise to anger Jethro."

"I understand. Is it all right if we pass this message on to people?"

"Yes, but do not bring more people."

"Agreed. I want to thank you for allowing me to get to know you."

"No one knows Jethro."

"I didn't mean to presume..."

"Jethro knows you have a good heart. You must remain."

"Remain? Me? Here?"

"You are needed here."

"I don't understand," Max said.

"You will."

These cryptic remarks signifying nothing rankled Max, who had plans to travel, lecture, and write. But he was getting the impression that his fate was tied to Eureka. This was brought home in dramatic fashion by Hurricane Bruno, a monster storm that was ravaging Houston as it came off the Gulf and was threatening everything in sight as it moved north. Eureka was in the bullseye as the track of the storm moved it closer and closer to the little community. Max was helping to prepare for the onslaught when he received a visit from...Jethro.

"Wh...what?"

"Will you stay?" Jethro asked.

"Stay? Here? No, I have plans to move on."

"Stay."

"Why?"

"If you stay, I will spare Eureka."

"You can do that?"

"There is much that Jethro can do."

"Let me see if I understand. If I promise to remain in Eureka, you will spare this hurricane that is about to beat down our doors?"

"Stay."

"OK. OK. I will stay. I kind of like it here anyway. Yes, I'll stay."

There were no other words as Jethro disappeared. But, much to the amazement of meteorologists, the category five hurricane did an unexpected detour as it approached Eureka and pounded the western part of Arkansas with torrential rain and destruction. But, Eureka received a half inch of much-needed rain, but no damage at all. It is an incident that has been studied many times, and no one can give a good explanation for it. But Max knew better.

"I can't explain this, but I know what I have to do." He explained everything to Priscilla, who was happy with the decision to remain in Eureka.

"I love it here. The people are good and kind, and we can have a good life here. We can still travel, Max. I think Jethro will understand that as long as our roots are here, we can have a good life."

"Sweetheart, as long as you are with me, I can make do in a tree hut. Did you get all of the video?"

"Yes, I did. Now, it's up to you how much you want to release."

"Right. Now the fun begins," he said with a devilish grin.

Epilogue: Legacy of the Guadian of the Ozarks

Max was able to keep the mystery going for three months after their final Jethro encounter. The footage continued to captivate both newspaper readers as well as those following with the news feeds to the networks. Max established a fund with a business manager who invested some of the donations and saw the fund's value double in the first five years.

As promised, Stan invited Max and Priscilla to a lavish reception in honor of their wedding. He had a very attractive woman on his arm who seemed to adore him. Doris was there too, with her Eddie, and wished Max and Priscilla well.

Max then holed himself up in a room at the Radisson and hammered out the complete story in two months. That led to a book deal that was in the high six figures. Offers of a movie were being discussed. And it was Stan's proud pleasure to offer Max's work to the Pulitzer committee. It would be two months before Max had his Pulitzer. After a stay in Grand Rapids, he and Priscilla returned 'home' to Eureka. They loved the simple life of the wonderful Ozark people. And they loved him, too.

His life could not be fuller until it was. Priscilla presented him with a son the first year they were back and four more children in the next eight years. Max and Priscilla made regular trips to Grand Rapids to see Stan. One such meeting was special. Max stood up as best man as Stan and the lovely Marissa Danforth tied the knot.

Stan was even prouder when he learned that Max founded a newspaper. Its circulation was limited to just the confines of Eureka, but Max's imaginative writing and editorials quickly established it as a force to be reckoned with. He named it the Eureka Gazette. Such was the influence of Max that politicians approached to kiss the ring of the man who could make or break a career. Max took his responsibility seriously and always elicited promises of reform.

So, the little man from Grand Rapids stood like a colossus in the little community of Eureka.

Did he ever see Jethro again? It is hard to say. But Max was known to take trips into the wilds and return with an energy that amazed everyone, even into his old age. Some believed he tapped into the fountain of youth. Others just believed he received a dose of Jethro.

Don't miss out!

Visit the website below and you can sign up to receive emails whenever "Joe Roberts" Caputo publishes a new book. There's no charge and no obligation.

https://books2read.com/r/B-A-MAVOC-XAYCF

BOOKS 2 READ

Connecting independent readers to independent writers.

Also by "Joe Roberts" Caputo

Jethro